THE OMEN

*To the Honorable
Jeremy Thorn, next
Ambassador of the
United States to the
Court of St. James in
London, and his wife
Katherine, the gift of
a son . . .*

DAMIEN . . .
*Heir to the Thorn
millions, a beautiful
child of a beautiful
family. Until dark
doubts and sudden,
violent death begin
to chip away at their
ordered world.*

WHO IS DAMIEN?

Other SIGNET Movie Tie-ins
You'll Enjoy Reading

THE OMEN

by
David Seltzer

Ⓢ
A SIGNET BOOK
NEW AMERICAN LIBRARY
TIMES MIRROR

Copyright © 1976 by Twentieth Century-Fox Film Corporation

SIGNET TRADEMARK REG. U.S. PAT. OFF. AND FOREIGN COUNTRIES
REGISTERED TRADEMARK—MARCA REGISTRADA
HECHO EN CHICAGO, U.S.A.

SIGNET, SIGNET CLASSICS, MENTOR, PLUME AND MERIDIAN BOOKS
are published by The New American Library, Inc.,
1301 Avenue of the Americas, New York, New York 10019

FIRST SIGNET PRINTING, JULY, 1976

13 14 15 16 17 18 19

PRINTED IN THE UNITED STATES OF AMERICA

Let He who hath understanding
Reckon the number of the Beast;
For it is a human number,
Its number is Six Hundred and Sixty-Six.

—BOOK OF REVELATIONS

Preface

It happened in a millisecond. A movement in the galaxies that should have taken eons occurred in the blinking of an eye.

At the Cape Hattie observatory a young astronomer sat stunned, reaching an instant too late to activate the camera that might have recorded it: the splintering of three constellations that produced the dark, glowing star. From Capricorn, Cancer, and Leo pieces had suddenly flown, finding each other with magnetic certainty, melding into a pulsating galactic ember. It grew brighter now and the constellations shuddered—or was it trembling hands on the eyepiece as the astronomer struggled to stifle his confused cry?

He feared he was alone with it, but in fact he was not. For from the very bowels of the earth there came a distant sound. It was the sound of voices; human, yet not, growing in devout cacophony with the heightening potency of the star. In caves, basements, and open fields they had gathered; midwives to the birth, some twenty thousand strong. With hands joined and heads bowed, their voices rose until the vibration could be heard and felt everywhere. It was the sound of the OHM, ringing upward to the heavens and inward to the pre-biblical core of the earth.

It was the sixth month, the sixth day, the sixth hour. The precise moment predicted by the Old Testament when earth history would change. The wars, the turmoil of recent centuries had been mere rehearsals, a testing of the climate to determine when mankind would be ready to be led. Under Caesar they had cheered while Christians were fed to the lions, and under Hitler while Jews were reduced to charred remains. Now democracy was fading, mind-impairing drugs had become a way of life, and in the few countries where freedom of worship was still allowed, it was widely proclaimed that God was dead. From Laos to Lebanon brother had turned against brother, fathers against children; school busses and marketplaces exploded daily in the growing din of preparatory lust.

Students of the Bible had seen it too, the falling into place of biblical symbols that heralded the event that was now at hand. In the form of the Common Market, the Holy Roman Empire had risen, and with the statehood of Israel the Jews had returned to the Promised Land. This, coupled with worldwide famine and the disintegration of international economic structure, demonstrated more than a mere coincidence of events. Clearly it was a *conspiracy* of events. The Book of Revelations had predicted it all.

As, high in the sky, the black star grew brighter, the chant grew louder, and the basalt center of the planet reverberated with its power. Within the hollowed-out ruins of the ancient city of Meggido, the old man Bugenhagen could feel it, and wept; his scrolls and tablets useless now. And above him on the desert floor outside of Israel the night shift of archaeological students paused in their work, their dirt-sifters falling silent as the ground beneath them began to tremble.

In his first-class seat aboard the 747 bound from Washington to Rome, Jeremy Thorn felt it too and routinely fastened his seat belt, preoccupied with what awaited him below. Even if he had known the reason for the sudden turbulence, it would have been too late. For at that moment, in the basement of the Ospedale Generale in Rome, a stone crushed the head of the child that was meant to be his.

Chapter One

At any given moment there are over a hundred thousand people in airplanes in the sky. It was the kind of statistic that intrigued Thorn, and as he read it in the *Skyliner* magazine he instantly cleaved the human population between those on the earth and those in the air. Normally he was given to more serious musing, but on this particular flight he grasped at anything to keep his mind off the uncertainty that he was heading for. What the statistic meant was that if suddenly the earthbound population were to be annihilated, there would be over a hundred thousand of them left aloft, sipping martinis and watching movies, unaware that all had been lost.

As his plane lumbered through the troubled skies over Rome, he wondered how many of them up there at this moment were male, and how many were female, and how, if they all found a safe haven to land in, they would go about reconstructing a society. Probably most were male, in the middle to upper economic bracket, which meant they would possess skills that were relatively useless if they returned to an earth where all the working men were gone. Managers with no one to manage, accountants with no one to account. It might be a good idea if a few planeloads of maintenance men and construction workers were kept aloft at all times so there would be ample muscle to begin again. Wasn't it Mao Tse-tung who said it? It is the country with the best maintenance men that would best survive a holocaust.

The plane's hydraulics wheezed beneath his feet and Thorn extinguished his cigarette, gazing out at the lights dimly visible below. With all his traveling in recent months this had become a familiar sight, but tonight it brought anxiety. The telegram he'd received in Washington was twelve hours old and by now whatever had happened was over. He would find Katherine fulfilled at last, in a hospital bed nursing their newborn child, or in a state of hopeless despair at having lost it once again. Unlike the other two pregnancies that had ended after just a few months, this one had gone all the way to eight. And if this time something went wrong, he knew that Katherine would be lost.

They had been together almost since childhood, he and Katherine, and even then at the age of seventeen, her instability was plain. The haunted eyes, begging for someone to protect her; the role of protector suiting his needs as well. It was this that formed the very core of their relationship, but in recent years as his responsibilities began to extend far beyond her, she had been left behind, lonely and isolated, unable to cope with the duties of a politician's wife.

The first signal of her distress had gone almost unnoticed, Thorn expressing anger instead of concern when he returned home to find she had taken a scissors and fairly butchered her hair. A Sassoon wig covered it until it grew out, but a year later he found her in their bathroom making small cuts in the end of her fingers with a razor blade, dismayed herself at why she was doing it. It was then that they sought help; a psychiatrist who merely sat in bland silence. She quit him after a month, deciding that all she needed was a child.

Impregnation occurred immediately, and the three months of that first pregnancy were the best they had ever known. Katherine looked and felt beautiful and even traveled to the Far East at her husband's side. The pregnancy ended in the lavatory of an airplane, blue water washing away her hope as she cried.

The second pregnancy took two years to accomplish and all but destroyed the sex life that had once been a pillar of their relationship. The fertility specialist had pinpointed the right moment in her estrus cycle at a time of day that was difficult for Thorn to be with her, and he had felt foolish and used as month after month he left his office to perform the perfunctory, mechanical task. It was even suggested that he masturbate so that his semen could be injected artificially, but here he drew the line. If a child were that important to her, she could adopt. But she would have none of it. The child had to be their own.

In the end one lonely cell found another, and for five and a half months hope again bloomed. This time the pains began in a supermarket and Katherine doggedly continued her shopping, trying to deny it until it could be denied no longer. It was a blessing, they said, because the fetus was impaired, but this only furthered her despair and she slipped into a depression that took six months to relieve. It was the third time now, and Thorn knew it was the last. If something went wrong this time, it would be the end of her sanity.

The plane touched down on the runway and there was a spattering of light applause, an open admission that the passengers were delighted, even somewhat surprised, to have made it back down alive. Why do we fly? wondered Thorn. Is life all that dispensable? He remained in his seat as others groped for their carryons, crushing toward the door. He would be VIP'd off, taken quickly through customs, into a waiting car. It was the nicest part of coming back to Rome, for here he was something of a celebrity. As the President's economic advisor, he was chairman of the World Economy Conference which had been moved from Zurich to Rome. The initial four-week agenda had droned on now for close to six months, and in that time the paparazzi had begun to notice him, the rumor spreading that in a few years hence he himself would be a U.S. Presidential hopeful.

At the age of forty-two, he was in his prime,

having carefully paved the way for what now seemed inevitable. His appointment as chairman of the Economy Conference put him in the public eye, providing a stepping-stone to an ambassadorship, a cabinet position, then, probably, elected office. That the man who was now President of the United States was once his college roommate was no hindrance, but actually Thorn had done it on his own.

The family industrial plants that boomed during the war had provided him with the best education money could buy and potentially a life of ease. But at his father's death he closed them down, defying his advisors in the vow never again to foster implements of destruction. All war is fratricide. It was Adlai Stevenson who said it, Thorn who quoted it, and in the interest of peace the Thorn fortune multiplied. Real estate holdings evolved into construction, Thorn becoming passionately involved with improving ghetto areas and dispensing small business loans to the capable and needy. It was this that made him unique; a gift for accumulating money and a sense of responsibility for those who had none. The estimate that his personal wealth was close to a hundred million dollars was unverifiable, and in truth Thorn himself did not know. To account would have meant to pause, and Jeremy Thorn was in constant motion.

As the taxi stopped short in front of the darkened Ospedale Generale, Father Spilletto gazed down from his second-floor office window, knowing in an instant that the man bounding out was Jeremy Thorn. The rugged jaw and graying temples were familiar from newspaper photos, the attire and gait seemed familiar as well. It was satisfying that Thorn looked every inch what he should. Plainly, the choice had been right. Drawing his robes around him, the priest stood, his enormous form dwarfing the small wooden desk before him, and, without expression, moved quietly to the door. Thorn's footsteps could already be heard below, entering, echoing as they moved vigorously across the bare, tiled floor.

"Mr. Thorn?"

Below him, Thorn turned, his eyes searching upward in the darkness.

"Yes?"

"I am Father Spilletto. I sent you . . ."

"Yes. I got your telegram. I left as soon as I could."

The priest moved into a shaft of light and started down the stairwell. There was something in his movement, the silence that surrounded it, that signaled all was not well.

"Is . . . the child born?" asked Thorn.

"Yes."

"My wife . . . ?"

"She is resting."

The priest was at the base of the stairwell now and his eyes met Thorn's, trying to prepare him, to soften the blow.

"Something's gone wrong," said Thorn.

"The child is dead."

There came an awesome silence, the empty tiled corridors seeming to ring with it, as Thorn stood paralyzed, as though hit by a body blow.

"It breathed but a moment," whispered the priest, "then breathed no more."

The priest watched, unmoving, as the man before him walked stiffly to a bench and sat for a long moment, then bowed his head and wept. The sound of weeping echoed through the corridors, and the priest waited his turn to speak.

"Your wife is safe," he said, "but she will be unable to bear another child."

"It will destroy her," whispered Thorn.

"You could adopt."

"She wanted her own."

In the silence that followed, the priest stepped

forward. His features were coarse but composed, the eyes filled with compassion. Only a trickle of perspiration betrayed the tension hidden within.

"You love her very much," he said.

Thorn nodded, unable to find his voice.

"Then you must accept God's plan."

From the shadows of a darkened corridor, an aged nun appeared, her eyes imploring the priest to join her. They came together, whispering for a moment in Italian before she departed and the priest turned again to Thorn. There was something in his eyes that made Thorn stiffen.

"God works in mysterious ways, Mr. Thorn." And he held out his hand. Thorn, rising, was compelled to follow.

The maternity ward was three floors up and they took a back stairwell, an avenue little used and lit only by bare bulbs. The ward itself was dark and clean, the smell of babies renewing the sense of loss that throbbed like a hammer deep in Thorn's stomach. Moving to a glass partition, the priest paused, waiting as Thorn hesitantly approached and gazed down at what lay on the other side. It was a child. Newborn. A child of angelic perfection. With thick black hair tousled above deep-set blue eyes it stared upward, instinctively finding Thorn's eyes.

"It is a foundling," said the priest. "Its mother died as your own child . . . in the same hour." Confused, Thorn turned to him. "Your wife needs a child," continued the priest. "The child needs a mother."

Thorn slowly shook his head. "We wanted our own," he said.

"If I may suggest . . . it very much resembles . . ."

And Thorn looked again, realizing it was true. The child's coloration was the same as Katherine's, the features resembled his own. The jaw was firm, it even had the unique Thorn cleavage in its chin.

"The Signora need never know," implored the priest.

And from Thorn's sudden silence, he took heart. Thorn's hand had begun to tremble and the priest took it, infusing him with confidence.

"Is . . . it a healthy child?" asked Thorn in a trembling voice.

"Perfect in every way."

"Are there relatives?"

"None."

Around them the empty corridors hissed with silence, a stillness so dense that it assaulted the ears.

"I am in full authority here," said the priest. "There will be no records. No one would know."

Thorn averted his eyes, desperate with indecision.

"Could I . . . see my own child?" he asked.

"What's to be gained?" implored the priest. "Give your love to the living."

And from behind the glass partition the infant lifted both arms toward Thorn as if in a gesture of desire.

"For the sake of your wife, Signor, God will forgive this deception. And for the sake of this child who will otherwise have no home . . ."

His voice fell to silence, for no more needed to be said.

"On this night, Mr. Thorn . . . God has given you a son."

In the night skies above them the black star reached its apex, suddenly shattered by an angry bolt of lightning. And in her hospital bed Katherine Thorn thought she was awakening naturally, unaware of the injection she had been given just moments before. She had suffered ten hours of labor and had felt the final contractions, but she slipped into unconsciousness before she could see the child. Now, as her faculties returned, she was gripped with fear but fought to calm herself as she heard footsteps approaching from the corridor outside. The door swung open and she saw her husband. And in his arms was a child.

"Our child," said Thorn, his voice trembling with emotion. "We've got our son."

She reached out and took the baby, and wept with joy. And as he watched through blurred eyes, Thorn thanked God for showing him the way.

Chapter Two

The Thorns were both of Catholic parentage, but neither of them was religious. Katherine was given to occasional prayer and visits to church on Christmas and Easter, but more out of superstition and sentiment than a belief in Catholic dogma. Thorn himself was lapsed and did not take seriously, as Katherine did, the fact that their son Damien was never christened. It wasn't that they didn't try. Immediately after his birth they dutifully brought the infant to church, but so abject was his terror upon entering the cathedral that they cut the ceremony short. The priest had followed them out to the street with water cupped in his hands, warning that if the child were not christened he could never enter the Kingdom of Heaven, but Thorn refused to continue, seeing clearly that the infant was in a state of terror. To satisfy Katherine they improvised a ceremony at home, but she was never totally reassured, intending one day to return with Damien and make sure it was done right.

That day never came, for they were swept into a whirlwind of distractions, and the christening was forgotten. The Economy Conference had ended and they moved back to Washington, Thorn resuming his duties as a Presidential advisor and becoming a political entity in his own right. Their rambling estate in McLean, Virginia, became the scene of gatherings that made the columns from New York to California, and the Thorn family became familiar to readers of national magazines all over the country. They were photogenic, they were rich, and they were on the way up. And, more important, they were often in the company of the President. It was plain that Thorn was being groomed, and it came as no surprise to political speculators when he was appointed Ambassador to the Court of St. James, a key position in which he could display his charismatic potential to advantage.

Returning to London, the Thorns took up quarters in the seventeenth-century mansion at Pereford. Life became a beautiful dream, for Katherine especially; so perfect it was almost frightening. At their country house she could remain in seclusion being nothing more than a mother to her adored child; then, when she chose, she could emerge to be her husband's hostess at diplomatic functions. Now that she had her child, she had everything, including her husband's adoration, and she blossomed like an orchid; fragile, yet in full flower, pleasing everyone with her freshness and beauty.

The Pereford mansion was elegant and steeped in English history. It had a cellar where an exiled duke had hidden until he was found and executed, and it was surrounded by a forest where King Henry V had hunted wild boar. There were secret passages and drafty crawlways; but mostly there was joy, for the house was filled with company and laughter at all hours of the day.

For household duties, there was a staff of day help as well as a permanent couple, the Hortons, very English, very dignified, who acted as cook and chauffeur. To entertain Damien when Katherine was occupied with official chores, there was a plump English girl named Chessa, no more than a child herself, but a delight to everyone and an indispensable addition to the family. She was bright and full of play, and adored Damien as though he were her own. They would often spend hours together, Damien toddling after her on the vast lawn or sitting quietly by the pond where she would catch tadpoles and dragonflies for them to bring home in jars.

The boy was growing into an artist's rendering of the ideal child. In the three years since his birth the promise of physical perfection had been fulfilled, and his health and strength were phenomenal too. He had a kind of composure, a contentment, that one rarely sees in the young, and visitors occasionally found themselves unnerved by his gaze. If intelligence could be measured by attention span, then he was a genius, for he would often sit for hours, positioned on a small wrought-iron bench beneath an apple tree, his eyes trained on the people who came and went, absorbing every detail of what took place before him. Horton, the chauffeur, occasionally took him out on errands, enjoying his silent presence, amazed by the child's fascination with everything that went on in the world.

"He's like a little man from Mars," Horton once remarked to his wife. "Like he was sent here to study the human race."

"He's the apple of his mother's eye," she responded. "Wouldn't do you no good to be heard saying that."

"I'm not downing him. Just that he is a bit unusual."

The only other troubling aspect about Damien was that he rarely used his voice. Joy was expressed with a wide, dimpled grin; sorrow with strangely silent tears. Katherine once mentioned this to her physician, but the doctor was most reassuring. He told the story of a child who never uttered a word until he was eight years old, and then only to remark that he didn't like mashed potatoes. When, in amazement, the mother asked him why, if he could speak, he'd never spoken before, the child replied that up until now she'd never served mashed potatoes.

Katherine had laughed at the story and relaxed about Damien. After all, Albert Einstein didn't speak until he was four, and Damien was only three and a half. Aside from being quiet and observant, he was in every way the perfect child, the appropriate issue of the perfect marriage of Jeremy and Katherine Thorn.

Chapter Three

The man named Haber Jennings was born an Aquarian; a textbook product of Uranus on the rise in conjunction with a waxing moon. He was ill-kempt and persistent to the point of embarrassment. Jennings was a paparazzi; one of the geeks of the journalism world, tolerated only because he was willing to do what none of the others would. Like a cat stalking a mouse he had been known to hole up for days waiting for a single photo: Marcello Mastroianni sitting on the toilet, taken with a long lens from the top of a eucalyptus tree; the Queen Mother having her corns removed; Jackie Onassis on her yacht, vomiting. These were his stock in trade. He knew where to be and when, his photos unlike any others in the trade. He lived in a one-room flat in Chelsea and seldom wore socks. But he researched his subjects with the thoroughness of Salk seeking the cure for polio.

Lately he had become fixated on the Ambassador to London, a prime target because of his perfect facade. Did the beautiful couple ever have sex? And if so, how? He sought to reveal what he called their *humanity*, but in truth he wanted to prove that everyone was as disgusting as himself. Did the Ambassador ever buy an obscene magazine and masturbate? Did he have any girls on the side? These were the questions that intrigued him, and though they would never be answered, there was always hope; this was the impetus that motivated him to watch and wait.

Today he would go to the Thorn estate in Pereford, probably not to photograph because there would be so many others, but just to get the layout, to find the right windows, the entrances and exits, determine which servants could be bought for a couple of pounds.

Rising early, he checked out his cameras, wiping the lenses with Kleenex, then squeezed a boil, using the same tissue to absorb the discharge. He was thirty-eight years old and still plagued with skin blemishes, this being no small factor in going through life with a camera in front of his face. His body was lean but without muscle tone, the only definition coming from the rumpled clothes that he pulled from a pile at the foot of his bed.

Before leaving, he set his darkroom timers, then shuffled through piles of papers looking for the engraved invitation. It was to be a birthday party. The fourth birthday of the Thorn child. From all the ghetto areas of London busloads of crippled children and orphans were already on the way to Pereford.

The drive through the English countryside was relaxing and Jennings lit up an opium joint to free his mind. After a while the road seemed to be moving beneath him, the car standing still, and he released his hold on reality, exploring the corners of his mind. His fantasies were still life, like the pictures he took. The subject was himself, always frozen in heroic gesture. Crossing an icepack with sled dogs, rubbing Coppertone on Sophia Loren.

For a mile outside the Thorn estate, policemen directed traffic and checked credentials; stuporously Jennings gazed straight ahead while they double-checked his invitation to make sure it was real. He was accustomed to this treatment and knew that all he had to do to avoid it was to appear presentable. But this was part of his ammunition. He could better observe people because they preferred to pretend he wasn't there.

Finally ushered through the great wrought-iron gates, Jennings blinked hard, trying to shake the opium illusions before he realized that the illusion was real.

The entire estate had been turned into a sumptuous carnival. The lawns were teeming with color and life, small bodies running between circus tents and carousels, while vendors moved through, hawking cotton candy and taffy apples, their voices lost in the waltz-wheeze of organ music that pumped children up and down on swans and pink horses. There was a fortune teller's booth with many of London's most important dignitaries queued up before it, Shetland ponies running free, even a baby elephant painted with red dots accepting peanuts from hordes of squealing children. Photographers ran everywhere, out of their minds with greed, but to Jennings there was nothing there to photograph. Only the facade. The brick wall that everyone else took for reality.

"What's the matter, mate? Run out of film?"

It was Hobie talking, the stringer for the *News Herald*, feverishly reloading beside the hot-dog table, as Jennings casually approached and took a handful of food.

"Just waiting for his canonization," Jennings replied with distaste.

"How's that?"

"I don't know if we've got just the heir to the Thorn millions here, or Jesus Christ himself."

"You're a fool to miss out, man. It's not often you'll get into a place like this."

"Why bother? What I need I can buy from you."

"You want an exclusive, do you?"

"No other way."

"Well, good luck, then. This is the most private family this side of Monaco."

The exclusive. That was the Jennings dream. Private entree into rarefied realms. There was excitement in the stalking to be sure, but no status, no respect. If he could somehow work his way *inside*; that's where it was at.

"Hey, Nanny! Nanny!" shouted Hobie in the dis-

16

tance. "Look this way!" And all attention focused on a towering birthday cake being wheeled out from inside.

The child's nanny, Chessa, was dressed as a clown, her face whitened with powder and painted with a garish red smile. As the photographers danced about her, she delighted in the attention, hugging, kissing, smearing her makeup onto the child.

"Can he blow them out?" they shouted. "Let him take a try."

Jennings' eyes traveled slowly through the crowds; he spotted the face of Katherine Thorn, standing at a distance, a vague hint of disapproval playing about her mouth. For a split second her mask was down, and Jennings instinctively reached for his camera, clicking off a shot. At the birthday cake a howl of applause and approval went up, as Katherine slowly moved forward.

"Tell his fortune!" shouted a reporter. "Take him to the fortune teller!" And as a body, the crowd began to move, bearing the nanny and her adored child across the lawn.

"I'll take him," said Katherine, reaching toward them as they passed.

"I can do it, mum," replied the nanny brightly.

"I'll do it," smiled Katherine.

And in the single moment as their eyes met, the nanny relinquished the child. It was a moment unnoticed by all, the momentum and noise carrying them forward, but Jennings was watching it through his viewfinder. As the crowd moved on, the nanny was left standing alone, the towering house framed behind her, the clown costume somehow accentuating her air of desertion. Jennings hit the button twice before the young girl turned and walked slowly back to the house.

At the fortune teller's tent Katherine admonished reporters to stay outside, then entered, breathing a sigh of relief at the sudden quiet and darkened atmosphere.

"Hello, little boy."

The words came from beneath a hood; an apparition

was seated behind a small green table, her voice strained to sound witchlike, her face made up in green. As Damien gazed down, he stiffened, climbing fast to his mother's shoulder.

"Come on, Damien," laughed Katherine, "this is a nice witch. Aren't you a nice witch?"

"Of course," laughed the fortune teller. "I won't hurt you."

"She's going to tell your fortune," coaxed Katherine.

"Come on," gestured the fortune teller. "Hold out your hand."

But Damien would not, clinging tightly to his mother. The fortune teller lifted her rubber mask, revealing herself to be just a plain young girl wearing an enormous grin.

"Look. I'm just a person. This won't hurt a bit."

Relaxing, Damien held out his hand, Katherine sitting with him, across the card-strewn table.

"Oh, what a nice, soft hand. This is going to be a good, good fortune."

But she paused, gazing at the hand with confusion.

"Let's try the other," she said.

As Damien held out his other hand, the girl gazed at both, clearly puzzled.

"Is this part of the routine?" asked Katherine.

"I've never seen this," said the girl. "I've been doing children's parties for three years, and I've never seen it before."

"Seen what?"

"Look. No personality lines. All he's got is creases."

"What?"

Katherine looked too.

"They look fine to me," she said.

"Was he in a fire?" the girl asked.

"Of course not."

"Look at your own hand. Look at all the tracing. It's different with each person. These are marks of our identity."

There passed an uncomfortable silence, the child himself gazing at his hands, wondering what was wrong.

"Look how smooth his fingertips are," said the girl. "I don't think he has any prints."

Katherine looked closely. She realized it was true.

"Well," laughed the girl, "if he robs a bank, they won't catch him."

And then she laughed harder, while Katherine gazed at the small hands in puzzled silence.

"Could you tell his fortune, please? That's what we came in for." Katherine's voice was uneasy.

"Of course."

But as the young girl reached for the child's hand, they were interrupted by a voice from outside. It was Chessa, the nanny. And she was shouting from a distance.

"Damien! Damien!" she cried. "Come out! I've got a surprise for you!"

The fortune teller paused, sensing, as Katherine did, a certain desperation in the cry.

"Damien! Come out and see what I'll do for you!"

Exiting from the tent with Damien in her arms, Katherine paused, gazing upward toward the house. There, poised on the roof was Chessa, a heavy rope in her hand, cheerfully stretching it upward to show it was wound around her neck. Beneath her the crowds began to turn, smiling in confused anticipation as the small clown moved forward to the edge and held her hands out as if readying a high dive into a pool of water.

"Look here, Damien!" she shouted. "It's all for you!"

And in a single movement she stepped off the roof, her body plummeting downward, snapped back up by the rope, then hanging limp. Silent. Dead.

On the lawn they stood in stunned silence, the small body swinging gently to the accompaniment of a carousel waltz. And then there was a scream. It was Katherine. It took four people to quiet her and move her into the house.

Left alone in his room, Damien gazed out over the empty lawn, only maintenance men and vendors left, staring upward in silence as a policeman grimly mounted a ladder and cut the body down. It slipped from his grip, falling headfirst onto a bricked patio. And it lay there crumpled, eyes gazing skyward, mouth painted in a garish grin.

The days before Chessa's funeral were painted in gloom. The skies above Pereford had turned to gray, reverberating with distant thunder, and Katherine spent most of her time sitting alone in the darkened living room, staring into space. A coroner's report had shown that there was a high amount of Benadryl, an allergy drug, in the girl's bloodstream when she died, but this only added to the confusion and speculation as to why she had taken her life. To avoid the reporters who would try to embellish the story, Thorn remained at home, his attention on his wife who was, he feared, slipping into that state he had seen a few years before.

"You're letting this get the best of you, you know," he said one night as he entered the living room. "It's not as though she were a member of our family."

"She was," replied Katherine quietly. "She told me she wanted to stay with us forever."

Thorn shook his head, unable to make any sense of it.

"I guess she changed her mind," he said. He hadn't meant to sound cold, but his words were harsh, and he was aware of Katherine's eyes finding his from across the room.

"I'm sorry," he added. "I hate to see you like this."

"It was my fault, Jeremy."

"Your fault?"

"There was a moment at the party."

Thorn crossed the room and sat beside her, his eyes etched with concern.

"She was getting a lot of attention," Katherine continued, "and I was jealous of it. I took Damien from her because I couldn't stand sharing center stage."

"I think you're being a little hard on yourself. The girl was deranged."

"And so am I," whispered Katherine, "if being in the limelight means so much to me."

Her voice fell to silence. There was nothing left to say. She slid into Thorn's arms and he held her until she slept. It was the kind of sleep he had seen before when she was taking Librium, and he wondered if the shock of Chessa's death had caused her to take it again. He sat there the better part of an hour before lifting her in his arms and carrying her into her room.

The following morning Katherine attended Chessa's funeral, taking Damien with her. It was a private affair conducted in a small cemetery on the outskirts of town, attended only by the girl's family, Katherine and Damien, and a balding priest who read from the scriptures while holding a folded newspaper over his head to ward off the persistent drizzle of rain. Fearing the publicity that would surround their attendance, Thorn had refused to go, entreating Katherine to do the same. But her need was plain. She had loved the girl and needed to put her to rest.

Outside the cemetery a group of reporters milled about, prevented from entering by two United States Marines, dispatched at the last minute by Thorn from his staff at the Embassy. Unseen among them was Haber Jennings, cloaked in black rain slicker and high boots, positioned in the far trees, scrutinizing the proceedings through a long-distance lens. It was no ordinary lens but a monstrous affair mounted on a tripod; a lens with which he could no doubt photograph two flies mating on the moon. With careful precision his telescopic viewer wandered from face to face: the family weeping; Katherine in a state of shock, the child beside her restless, his eyes roaming the bleak terrain.

It was the child who captured Jennings' interest, and he waited patiently for precisely the right moment to snap his shutter. It came in an instant. A flickering of the eyes and a sudden change of expression as though the boy had been suddenly frightened, then, just as suddenly, soothed. With his eyes riveted on a point far across the cemetery, his small body relaxed, somehow warmed in the midst of the cold, drizzling rain. Swinging his telescopic viewer, Jennings searched the landscape finding nothing but headstones. And then something moved. A dark, blurred object slowly coming into focus as Jennings adjusted his lens. It was an animal. A dog. Large and black, its pointed face distinguished by narrow-set eyes and a lower jaw that protruded forward, exposing teeth, stark against midnight fur. Unseen by all others, it sat motionless as statuary, its attention fixed firmly ahead. Jennings cursed himself for having loaded black and white, for the yellowed eyes added the perfect touch of eeriness to the scene. He opened his aperture so they'd expose stark white, then swung back to the boy, doing the same.

It was a morning well worth the effort, and as he packed his gear Jennings felt satisfied. But somehow he was uneasy too. At the top of a hill he gazed back to see the coffin being lowered into the grave. The child and the dog were small in the distance, but their silent communion was plain.

The following day brought a fresh onslaught of rain and the arrival of Mrs. Baylock. She was Irish and outrageous, pulling up to the front gates of Pereford and announcing herself as the new nanny. The guard had attempted to detain her but she bullied her way through, her boisterous manner at once intimidating and appealing.

"I know it's a difficult time for you," she announced

to the Thorns as she took off her coat in the vestibule, "so I won't impose on your grief. But between you and me, anyone who hires such a skinny young thing for a nanny is just asking for trouble."

The movements of her massive frame were so vigorous that they created a breeze; Thorn and Katherine, watching dumbfounded, were silenced by her certainty.

"You know how to tell a good nanny?" she laughed. "By the size of her breasts. These little girls with pigeon tits, they come and go in a week. But me, the big saggy ones like me. These are the nannies that stay. Go look in Hyde Park, you'll see it's true."

She paused only to pick up her suitcase.

"Well, now. Where's the boy?"

"I'll show you," said Katherine, indicating the stairs.

"Why don't you just leave us alone at first? Let us get acquainted in our own way."

"He's a little shy with new people."

"Not with me, he won't be, I can assure you of that."

"I really think . . ."

"Nonsense. Let me give it a try."

And in a moment she was climbing the stairs, her massive bottom disappearing from view. In the sudden silence left in her wake the Thorns exchanged a glance, Thorn nodding an uncertain approval.

"I like her," he said.

"I do, too."

"Where did you find her?"

"Where did *I* find her?" asked Katherine.

"Yes."

"*I* didn't find her. I assumed you found her."

And after a moment's pause, Thorn called up the stairs.

"Mrs. Baylock?"

"Yes?"

She was already on the second-story landing, her face peering down from above.

"I'm sorry . . . we're a little confused."

"Why is that?"

"We don't know how you got here."

"By taxi. I sent it away."

"No, no. I mean . . . who *called* you?"

"The agency."

"The agency?"

"They saw in the papers you'd lost your first nanny, so they sent you another."

It seemed a bit opportunistic, but knowing the fierce competition for employment in London, Thorn thought it made sense.

"Very enterprising," he said.

"Can I call to confirm that?" asked Katherine.

"Go right ahead," replied the woman. "You want me to wait outside in the rain?"

"No, no . . ." added Thorn quickly.

"Do I look like a foreign agent to you?" asked Mrs. Baylock.

"I don't think so," chuckled Thorn.

"Don't be so sure," the heavyset woman rejoined. "Maybe my girdle is filled with tape recorders. Why don't you send up a young Marine to check it out?"

They all laughed, Mrs. Baylock hardest of all.

"Go ahead," said Thorn, "we'll check it out later."

The Thorns retired to the drawing room where Katherine called the agency and confirmed Mrs. Baylock's credentials. She was well qualified with high recommendations, the only confusion being that their files showed she was presently employed in Rome. It was likely, however, that her situation had changed without being entered in their files, and they would clear that up as soon as the agency manager who no doubt sent her to the Thorns, returned from his four-week holiday. Katherine hung up the phone and gazed at her husband and both shrugged, rather pleased with what had transpired. Mrs. Baylock was an oddball, but full

24

of life, and that, more than anything, was what they needed.

Upstairs, Mrs. Baylock's smile had faded and she gazed down through misted eyes at the child asleep in his bed. He had apparently had his chin on the window ledge, watching the rain, and had slipped into slumber there, his hand still touching the pane. As the woman watched him, her chin began to tremble as though she were standing before an object of incomparable beauty. The child heard her faltering breath, his eyes opening slowly to meet hers. He stiffened and sat upright, edging back toward the pane.

"Fear not, little one," she whispered in a faltering voice. "I am here to protect thee."

Outside there came a sudden clap of thunder. The beginning of a two-week rain.

Chapter Four

By July the English countryside was in full flower, an unusually extended rainy season causing the Thames tributaries to overflow and bring life to even the most long-dormant seeds. The grounds of Pereford too had responded, becoming lush and green, the forested area beyond the gardens grown thick, sheltering an abundance of animal life. Horton feared that the rabbits of the forest would soon overrun their refuge and start feeding on the tulips, and he set traps for them; their piercing cries could be heard in the dead of night. The practice ended, not only because Katherine asked that he stop, but also because he had become uneasy about entering the forest to collect their remains. He felt "eyes" upon him, he said, as though he were being watched from the thickets. When he confessed this to his wife, she laughed, telling him it was probably the ghost of King Henry the Fifth. But Horton was unamused, refusing to enter the forest ever again.

It was, therefore, of special concern to him that the new nanny, Mrs. Baylock, often took Damien there, finding God-knows-what to amuse him with for hours at a time. Horton also noticed, on helping his wife sort through the laundry, that the boy's clothing had a great many dark hairs on them, as though he had been playing with an animal. But he failed to make any connection between the animal hairs and the trips into the Pereford forest, chalking it up to just another one of the disturbing aspects of Pereford House, of which there were coming to be many.

For one thing Katherine was spending less and less time with her child, somehow replaced by the new, exuberant nanny. It was true that Mrs. Baylock was a devoted governess and that the child had come to love her as well. But it was disquieting, even unnatural, that the boy preferred her company to that of his own mother. The entire staff had noticed it and talked about it, feeling hurt for their mistress's sake that she had been replaced in her child's affections by an employee. They wished that Mrs. Baylock would leave. But instead each day found her more firmly entrenched, exerting more influence on the masters of the house.

As for Katherine, she felt much the same way, but found herself helpless, unwilling to allow jealousy to again interfere with someone's affection for her child. She felt responsible for once having robbed Damien of a cherished companion, and she was loath to let it happen again. When, after the second week, Mrs. Baylock asked to move her sleeping quarters to a room directly opposite Damien's, Katherine consented. Perhaps among the rich this was how it was supposed to be. Katherine herself had been raised in more modest circumstances where it was a mother's job, and her only job, to be the companion and protector of her child. But life was very different here. She was the mistress of a great house, and perhaps it was time she started behaving that way.

Her newfound freedom was occupied in all the right ways; ways her husband heartily approved of. Mornings were taken up with charity causes, afternoons devoted to politically oriented teas. Thorn's wife was no longer the social oddball, the fragile flower, but a lioness possessed of an energy and confidence he had never seen before. This was the wife he had dreamed of for himself, and although the sudden change in personality was somehow disquieting, he did nothing to stand in her way. Even her lovemaking had changed, becoming more exciting, more passionate; Thorn failed to realize that it was possibly an expression of desperation rather than desire.

Thorn's own work was all-consuming; his job in London put him in a pivotal position in dealing with the oil crisis, and the President relied more and more on his feedback from informal meetings with the Saudi Arabian oil sheiks. A trip was planned to Saudi Arabia in the weeks ahead, and he would be going alone, since the Arabs took the presence of a wife in a touring entourage as a sign of weakness in a man.

"I don't understand it," said Katherine when he told her.

"It's a cultural thing," Thorn replied. "I'm going to their country, I have to respect it."

"Don't they have to respect you, too?"

"Of course they do."

"Well, I'm a cultural thing, too!"

"Katherine—"

"I've seen those sheiks. I've seen the women they buy. Wherever they go, they're followed by whores. Is that what they want you to do, too?"

"Frankly, I don't know."

They were in the bedroom and it was late. Not the time to start an argument.

"What do you mean by that?" asked Katherine quietly.

"It's an important trip, Kathy."

"So if they want you to sleep with a whore—"

"If they want me to sleep with their *eunuch*, I'll sleep with their *eunuch*. Do you know what's at stake here?"

They were at a standoff; Katherine slowly found her voice.

"Where am I in all this?" she asked quietly.

"You're here," he answered. "What you're doing is equally important."

"Don't patronize me."

"I'm trying to make you understand . . ."

"That you can save the world by doing what they say."

"That's one way of putting it."

She looked at him in a way that she never had before. Hard. Hateful. He felt weakened by her glare.

"I guess we're all whores, Jeremy," she said. "You're theirs and I'm yours. So let's just go to bed."

He spent a long time in the bathroom hoping she would be asleep by the time he came out. But she was not. She was awake and waiting, and he detected the scent of perfume in the air. He sat on the bed and gave her a long look; she returned a smile.

"I'm sorry," she said. "I do understand."

She took his face in her hands and pulled him close to her, locking him tightly in an embrace. Her breath became heavy and he began to make love to her, but she failed to move beneath him.

"Do it," she insisted. "Just do it to me. Don't go away."

And they made love in a way they had never made love before. Katherine refused to move, but refused to release him, urging him to completion with only her voice. When it was finished she released her hold and he moved off her, gazing at her with hurt and confusion.

"Go save the world now," she whispered. "Go do what they say."

Thorn did not sleep that night, sitting instead by the French doors in their room, gazing out into the moonlit night. He could see the forest from there, and it was unmoving, like a single entity in slumber.

Yet it was not slumbering, for he felt somehow as if it were staring back. They kept a pair of binoculars on the porch for bird watching; Thorn went out and got them, raising them to his eyes. At first all he saw was darkness. And then he spotted the eyes, gazing back. Two dark, glowing embers reflecting in the light of the moon; close-set, yellow, they were riveted on the house. It made him shudder and he lowered the binoculars, backing inside. He remained there, frozen for a moment, then forced himself to move; he padded silently down the long stairwell in his bare feet to the front door, then stepped quietly out. It was silent, even the noise of the crickets had stopped. Then he began to move again, as though pulled forward to the edge of the forest, where he paused, staring in. There was nothing. Not a sound. The two glowing embers were gone. Turning, his bare foot stepped on something soft and wet, and he sucked in his breath, stumbling to one side. It was a dead rabbit, still warm, its blood staining the grass where the head should have been.

The following morning he rose early, questioning Horton as to whether he was still setting traps for rabbits. Horton said he was not, and Thorn took him to the place where the dead carcass lay. It was buzzing with flies now, and Horton shooed them off as he knelt to examine it.

"What do you figure?" asked Thorn. "Do we have a predator in there?"

"Couldn't say, sir. But I doubt it."

He lifted the stiffened body, pointing to it with distaste.

"The head's what they *leave*, not what they *take*. Whatever killed this did it for fun."

Thorn instructed Horton to dispose of the body and to say nothing of it to anyone in the house. As they headed away, Horton stopped.

"I don't like that forest much, sir. And I don't like Mrs. Baylock taking your boy in there."

"Tell her not to," replied Thorn. "There's plenty to do here on the lawn."

That afternoon Horton did as he was told, and it brought the first indication to Thorn that something in the house was amiss. Mrs. Baylock sought him out in the drawing room that night and expressed irritation at having orders relayed to her through another member of the staff.

"It's not that I don't follow orders," she said indignantly, "it's just that I expect to receive them direct."

"I don't see what difference it makes," replied Thorn, and he was surprised at the anger that flashed in the woman's eyes.

"It's just the difference between a great house and a small house, Mr. Thorn. I get the feeling here that no one's in charge."

Turning on her heel, she left him alone; Thorn wondered what she meant. As far as the household was concerned, Katherine was in charge. But then again, he was away every day. Perhaps Mrs. Baylock was trying to tell him that things were not as they appeared. That Katherine was, in fact, not in control.

In his cramped six-flight walk-up in Chelsea, Haber Jennings was awake, gazing at the growing gallery of Thorn portraits that adorned his darkroom wall. There were the funeral pictures, dark and moody, the close-up of the dog among the headstones, the close-up of the boy. And then there were the pictures of the birthday party: Katherine watching the nanny, the nanny in clown costume, all alone. It was the latter photograph that most interested him, for above the nanny's head there was a kind of blemish, a photographic imperfection that somehow added to the portent of the scene. It was a fleck of faulty emulsion, a vague haze that hung over the nanny, forming a halo around her head and neck. Though normally a flawed photo would have been discarded, this one was worth keeping. The knowledge of what happened immediately after it was taken gave the blemish a symbolic quality—the shapeless form like a shadow of doom. The final photograph was of her dead body suspended by a rope; a jarring reality to complete the montage. Altogether the Thorn gallery

31

was a photographic study in the macabre. And it delighted Jennings. He had taken the same subjects that adorned the pages of *Good Housekeeping* and found something extraordinary in them, something different that no one had found before. He had also begun to research, using a contact in America to check into the Thorns' backgrounds for more information on them.

He found that Katherine had come from Russian immigrant parentage and that her natural father had died by his own hand. According to a back issue of the *Minneapolis Times*, he had leaped from the roof of a downtown Minneapolis office building. Katherine was born a month later and her mother remarried within a year, moving to New Hampshire with her new husband who gave the child his name. In a few interviews that Katherine had given out over the years there was never any mention of the stepfather, and Jennings speculated that she herself might not know the truth. It wasn't important, but somehow it gave Jennings an edge. Just one more delightful morsel, adding to the illusion that he was on the inside.

The only shot missing was that of the Ambassador himself, and Jennings hoped that tomorrow might be the day. There was an important wedding at All Saints Church which the Thorn family would be likely to attend. It wasn't Jennings' kind of setup, but he'd been lucky so far and perhaps would be again.

The day before the wedding Thorn dispensed with his customary Saturday chores at the Embassy and took Katherine for a drive in the country instead. He had been deeply disturbed by their argument and the strange lovemaking that had followed it, and he wanted to be alone with her to attempt to sort out what was going wrong. It appeared to be the right medicine, for she seemed relaxed for the first time in months, enjoying the drive, the simplicity of holding his hand as they wound their way through the English countryside. At noon they found themselves at Stratford-Upon-

Avon and attended a matinee performance of *King Lear*; Katherine sat enrapt, the play moving her to tears. Lear's soliloquy over the death of his child: "Why does a dog, a rat, have breath . . . and Thou no breath at all. . . ." struck a chord deep within her, and she wept openly, Thorn comforting her in the silence of the theater long after the play was over.

They returned to the car and drove on; Katherine held tightly to Thorn's hand, the release of emotions having created an intimacy that had long been absent in their relationship. She was vulnerable now, and as they stopped by a stream her tears came again. She spoke of her fears, her fears of losing Damien. She said that if anything happened to him, she would not be able to carry on.

"You won't lose him, Kathy," Thorn gently assured her. "Life couldn't be that cruel."

It was the first time he had called her Kathy in a long while, and it stung, somehow accentuating the distance that had come between them in recent months. They sat on the grass beneath a towering oak tree and Katherine's voice came in a whisper as she watched the movement of the stream.

"I'm so afraid," she said.

"There's nothing to be afraid of."

"Yet I fear everything."

A June bug was crawling beside her and she watched it wind its way across the vast landscape of grass.

"What's to fear, Katherine?"

"What isn't to fear?"

He gazed at her, waiting for more.

"I fear the good because it will go away . . . I fear the bad because I'm too weak to withstand it. I fear your success and I fear your failure. And I fear that I have little to do with either. I fear you'll become President of the United States, Jeremy . . . and you'll be saddled with a wife who isn't up to it."

"You've done beautifully," he reassured her.

"But I've hated it."

The admission was so simple, yet it had never been said. And it somehow cleansed them.

"Doesn't that shock you?" she asked.

"A little," he replied.

"You know what I want for us more than anything?" she asked.

He shook his head.

"I want for us to go back home."

He lay back in the grass, staring up into the leaves of the great oak.

"More than anything, Jeremy. To go where it's safe. To be where I belong."

A long silence followed; she lay beside him, nestled in his arms.

"It's safe here," she whispered. "In your arms."

"Yes."

She closed her eyes, her mouth upturning in a wistful smile.

"This is New Jersey, isn't it?" she whispered. "And isn't our little farm just over that hill? The one we've retired to?"

"It's a big hill, Kathy."

"I know. I know. We'll never get over it."

A slight breeze rose, rustling the leaves above them, and they watched in silence as rays of sunlight played on their faces.

"Maybe Damien will," whispered Thorn. "Maybe he's a budding young farmer."

"Not likely. He's your son through and through."

Thorn was unresponsive; his eyes were fixed on the leaves.

"He is, you know," Katherine mused. "It's as if I had nothing to do with him at all."

Thorn raised himself on one arm and regarded her saddened expression.

"Why do you say that?" he asked.

She shrugged, not knowing quite how to explain it.

"He's his own man. He doesn't seem to need anybody."

"He just seems that way."

"He's not attached to me like a child is to his mother. Were you attached to your mother?"

"Yes."

"Are you attached to your wife?"

Thorn's eyes met hers and he caressed her face; she kissed his hand.

"I don't ever want to leave this spot," she whispered. "I want to stay here like this."

And she moved her face upward until her lips touched his.

"You know, Kathy," Thorn whispered after a long silence, "when I first met you, I thought you were the most beautiful woman I'd ever seen."

She smiled at the memory and nodded her head.

"I still think so, Kathy," he whispered. "I still do."

"I love you," she whispered.

"I love you so," he responded.

Her mouth tightened, moisture tracing the rims of her closed eyes.

"I almost wish you would never to speak to me again," she whispered. "That's what I want to remember hearing you say."

And when she next opened her eyes, darkness was upon them.

When they returned to Pereford that night, everyone was asleep; they built a large fire in the fireplace, poured themselves wine, and sat snuggled together, deep in a soft leather couch.

"Can we do this in the White House?" Katherine asked.

"That's a long way off."

"Can we do this there?"

"Don't see why not."

"Can we be disgusting in the Lincoln bedroom?"

"Disgusting?"

"Carnal."

"In the Lincoln bedroom?"

"Right in his bed?"

"If Lincoln will move over, I guess."

"Oh, he can join in."

Thorn chuckled and pulled her close.

"Have to do something about the tourists, though," added Katherine. "They come through the Lincoln bedroom three times a day."

"We'll lock the door."

"Hell, no. Let's just charge them extra."

He laughed again, delighting in her mood.

"What a tour!" she whispered enthusiastically. "See the President screwing his wife."

"Kathy!"

"Kathy and Jerry, going at it. And old Lincoln rolling in his grave."

"What's gotten into you?" he gasped.

"You," she hissed.

He gazed at her, somewhat perplexed.

"Is this *you*?" he asked.

"The real me."

"The real you?"

"Aren't I disgusting?"

She laughed at herself, and so did he. And for that day and night it was the way she had dreamed it could be.

The following morning dawned bright, and by 9:00 A.M. Thorn was dressed for the wedding and moving jauntily down the stairs.

"Kathy?" he called.

"Not ready," her voice replied from upstairs.

"We're going to be late."

"That's true."

"They might *wait* for us, you know. We ought to make an effort."

"I'm making an effort."

"Is Damien dressed?"

"Hope so."

"I don't want to be late."

"Ask Mrs. Horton to make us some toast."

"I don't want any toast."

"I want some toast."

"Hurry up."

Outside, Horton had already pulled the limousine into place; Thorn stepped out and gave him a wait-a-minute signal, then moved quickly to the kitchen.

Katherine hurried from her room, tying the sash on her white dress, and moved toward Damien's, calling ahead of her as she went.

"Let's go, Damien. We're all ready!"

She stopped in his room, for he was nowhere in sight. She heard the sound of bathwater running in the tub and quickly entered the bathroom. She gasped in dismay. Damien was still in the bath, Mrs. Baylock washing him as he played.

"Mrs. Baylock," moaned Katherine, "I told you to have him dressed and ready . . ."

"If you don't mind, ma'am, I think he'd rather go to the park."

"I told you we were taking him to church!"

"Church is no place for a little boy on such a sunny day."

The woman was smiling, apparently feeling it didn't matter.

"Well, I'm sorry," replied Katherine evenly. "It's important that he go to church."

"He's too young for church. He'll just cause a fuss."

There was something in her tone and manner, perhaps too calm and innocent as she openly defied her, that set Katherine's teeth on edge.

"You don't seem to understand," said Katherine firmly. "I want him to accompany us to church."

Mrs. Baylock tensed, offended by Katherine's tone of voice. The child felt it too, moving closer to his nanny as she gazed up at his mother from her position on the floor.

"Has he been to church before?" Mrs. Baylock asked.

"I don't see what that has to do . . ."

"Kathy?!" called Thorn from downstairs.

"In a minute!" she called back.

She gazed harshly at Mrs. Baylock; the woman gazed back calmly.

"Get him dressed at once," said Katherine.

"Excuse me for speaking my mind, but do you really expect a four-year-old to understand the gibberish of a Catholic wedding?"

Katherine sucked in her breath.

"I am Catholic, Mrs. Baylock, and so is my husband."

"I guess someone has to be," the woman retorted. Katherine stood stunned, outraged by the open defiance.

"You will have my son dressed," she said tightly, "and in the car in five minutes time. Or you can start looking for another job."

"Maybe I'll do that anyway."

"If you choose."

"I'll think about it."

"I hope you do."

There was a tense silence, then Katherine turned on her heel to leave.

"About going to church . . . ?" Mrs. Baylock said.

"Yes?"

"You'll be sorry you took him."

Katherine left the room; within five minutes, Damien appeared, dressed and ready, at the car.

The drive carried them through Shepperton where

the new highway was being constructed, creating a massive traffic jam, which added to the charged silence within the Thorn limousine.

"Something wrong?" asked Thorn as he observed Katherine's expression.

"Not really."

"You look angry."

"Didn't mean to."

"What's it about?"

"Nothing much."

"Come on. Out with it."

"Mrs. Baylock," said Katherine with a sigh.

"What about her?"

"We had some words."

"About what?"

"She wanted to take Damien to the park."

"Something wrong with that?"

"Instead of church."

"Can't say I disagree."

"She did everything she could to keep him from coming."

"She's probably lonely without him."

"I don't know if that's good."

Thorn shrugged, gazing at the construction beside the car as they inched along in the snarled line of traffic.

"Can't we get around this, Horton?" he asked.

"No, sir," Horton replied, "but if you don't mind, I'd like to speak my piece about Mrs. Baylock."

Thorn and Katherine exchanged a glance, surprised at Horton's request.

"Speak away," said Thorn.

"I hate to do it around the little one."

Katherine looked at Damien, who was playing with the laces of his new shoes and apparently oblivious of the conversation.

"It's all right," said Katherine.

"I think she's a bad influence," said Horton. "She's got no respect for the rules of the house."

"What rules?" asked Thorn.

"I didn't want to go into specifics, sir."

"Please."

"Well, for one thing, it's accepted that the staff eats meals together and takes turns washing the dishes."

Thorn glanced at Katherine. Obviously it was nothing serious.

"She never eats with us," continued Horton. "She apparently comes down when we're all finished and takes a meal by herself."

"I see," said Thorn, feigning concern.

"And she leaves her dishes for the morning help to do."

"I think we can ask her to stop that."

"It's also expected that after lights-out the staff stays inside," continued Horton, "and I've seen her on more than one occasion in the small hours of the morning going into the forest outside. It was still dark out. And she was definitely walking quiet so no one would hear."

The Thorns pondered all this, both puzzled.

"Seems strange . . ." muttered Thorn.

"This part's indelicate and you'll have to excuse me," continued Horton. "But we've noticed she doesn't use any bathroom paper. By the toilet, you know? We haven't had to change it since she arrived."

In the back seat, the Thorns again glanced at each other. The story was getting bizarre.

"I add two and two," said Horton. "I think she does it in the forest. And I think that's uncivilized. It is if you ask me."

There followed a silence; the Thorns were perplexed.

"One more thing, sir. One more thing that's very wrong."

"What's that, Horton?" asked Thorn.

"She uses the telephone and she calls long distance to Rome."

Finished with what he had to say, Horton resumed his driving, finding a gap in the traffic and quickly pulling away. As the landscape moved by them, Katherine and Thorn pondered in silence, eventually finding each other's eyes.

"She was openly defiant today," said Katherine.

"You want to dismiss her?"

"I don't know. Do you?"

Thorn shrugged.

"Damien seems to enjoy her."

"I know."

"That counts for something."

"Yes," sighed Katherine. "I guess it does."

"You can let her go if you want."

Katherine paused, gazing out the window.

"I think perhaps she'll go on her own."

Sitting between them, Damien stared at the floor, his eyes unmoving as they sailed toward town.

All Saints Church was a mammoth building. Seventeenth-century architecture, melded with eighteenth, nineteenth, and twentieth in an ongoing flow of construction. The massive front doors were always open, the inside lighted day and night. Today the staircase leading to the doors was knee-deep in iris, and morning-coated ushers creating a stately path. The event had brought a crowd of people, some of them carrying picket signs with Communist party slogans, obvious defectors from a rally in Piccadilly who preferred to gawk here instead. The one great leveler for people of all stations and political persuasion was the presence of celebrities. People were gathered there in swarms; the crowd was beginning to burgeon, and security guards were having difficulty holding them back. It delayed the proceedings, and the arriving limousines had to queue up in single file and wait until they were directly in front of the church before they could discharge their passengers.

The Thorn limousine was a late arrival, taking its position near the end of the block. The security forces were thin here, and people crowded around the car, staring in unabashedly. As they inched through, the mob thickened, and Damien, who had dozed, began to rouse, startled and confused by the faces peering in. Katherine pulled him close, gazing uneasily ahead, but the bodies around them multiplied and began to push; the grotesque face of a hydrocephalic shoved close to the window beside Katherine and began to knock as though trying to get inside.

She turned to the face and flinched, for the man had begun to laugh, emitting a cascade of drool.

"Good lord," she gasped. "What is going on?"

"It's jammed up here for a good long block," replied Horton.

"Can't you get around it?" Katherine asked.

"We're bumper to bumper, front and back."

The knocking continued beside her and she closed her eyes, trying to shut out the sound, but it only grew, as others outside became amused by it and began to knock on the other windows as well.

"Look up ahead," said Horton. "Communists."

"Can't we get out of here?" begged Katherine.

And beside her Damien's eyes began to register fear, picking up his mother's alarm.

"It's all right ... it's all right," soothed Thorn, seeing the fear in the child's eyes. "These people can't hurt us, they just want to see who's inside."

But the child's eyes began to widen, and they were not focused on the people but on a point high above them; the towering spires of the church.

"There's nothing to be afraid of, Damien," said Thorn. "We're just going to a wedding."

But the child's fear grew, his face gripped with tension as they inched inexorably closer to the massive, towering church.

"Damien . . ."

Thorn glanced at Katherine, directing her eyes to the child. His face was stony, his body tightening as the crowds slid away and the cathedral suddenly loomed into view.

"It's all right, Damien," whispered Katherine, "the people are gone . . ."

But his eyes were riveted to the church, growing wider with each moment.

"What's wrong with him?" asked Thorn quickly.

"I don't know."

"What is it, Damien?"

"He's frightened to death."

Katherine gave him her hand and he clutched at it, gazing desperately into her eyes.

"It's a church, darling," said Katherine intensely.

As the boy turned, his lips went dry; the panic welling up within him as he began to pant, his face draining of color.

"My God," gasped Katherine.

"Is he ill?"

"He's like ice. He's cold as ice!"

The limousine stopped suddenly in front of the church and the door swung open; the usher's hand reaching in for Damien sent him into instant panic. Grabbing at Katherine's dress, he clung hard, beginning to whimper with fear.

"Damien!" cried Katherine. "Damien!"

As she tried to pull him off, he clung tighter, becoming more desperate as she fought to pull him off.

"Jeremy!" cried Katherine.

"Damien!" shouted Thorn.

"He's tearing my dress!"

Thorn reached for him, pulling forcefully, the child fighting harder to cling to his mother, his hands clawing her face and pulling her hair in his desperation to hold on.

"Help! God!" screamed Katherine.

"Damien!" shouted Thorn as he pulled futilely on the child. "Damien! Let go!"

As the child began to scream in terror, a crowd gathered around to watch their desperate struggle. Trying to help, Horton raced from the front seat, grabbing Damien and trying to pull him out the door. But the child had become an animal, shrieking as his fingers dug deep into Katherine's face and head, ripping a handful of hair.

"Get him off!" she screamed.

In terror she began beating at him, trying to wrest the fingers that had dug into her eye. In a sudden move, Thorn ripped Damien off her, grabbing him in a bear hug and pinning his arms to his side.

"Drive!" he panted to Horton. "Get out of here!"

And as the child struggled, Horton ran to the front seat, slamming doors as he went; the limousine lurched forward suddenly as it pulled quickly away from the curb.

"My God." sobbed Katherine, holding her head, "my . . . God. . . ."

And as the limousine sped away, the child's struggling slowly ceased, his head falling back in utter exhaustion. Horton swerved back onto the highway, and in a few moments, all was silent. Damien sat with glazed eyes, his face wet with perspiration; Thorn still clutched him in his arms, gazing fearfully ahead. Beside him, Katherine was in a state of shock, her hair pulled and torn, one eye swollen and nearly shut. They drove home in silence. No one dared to speak.

When they arrived at Pereford, they took Damien to his room and sat with him in silence as he stared out the window. His forehead was cool, so there was no need for a doctor. But he would not look at them; fearful, himself, of what he had done.

"I'll take care of him," Mrs. Baylock said quietly as she entered the room.

As Damien turned and saw her, his entire posture registered relief.

"He had a fright," Katherine said to the woman.

"He doesn't like church," replied the woman. "He wanted to go to the park instead."

"He became . . . wild," said Thorn.

"He was angry," said Mrs. Baylock. And she moved forward, lifting him into her arms. He clung to her. Like a child to his mother. The Thorns watched in silence. And then they slowly left the room.

"There's somethin' wrong," said Horton to his wife.

It was night now and they were in the kitchen, she having listened in silence as he recounted the day's events.

"There's somethin' wrong with that Mrs. Baylock," he continued, "and there's somethin' wrong with that boy, and there's somethin' wrong with this house."

"You're making too much of it," she replied.

"If you'd seen it, you'd know what I'm saying."

"A child's tantrum."

"An animal's tantrum."

"He's spirited, that's all."

"Since when?"

She shook her head as if to dismiss it, taking a pile of vegetables from the refrigerator and beginning to cut them into small pieces.

"Ever looked into them eyes?" asked Horton. "It's the same as lookin' into an animal's. They just watch. They wait. They know somethin' you don't know. They been someplace you never been."

"You and your hobgoblins," she muttered as she cut.

"You wait and see," assured Horton. "Something bad's happening here."

"Something bad is happening everywhere."

"I don't like it," he said darkly. "I'm thinking we should leave."

At the same moment the Thorns were on the patio. It was late now and Damien was asleep; the house was quiet and dark around them. Classical music was playing softly on the hi-fi, and they sat without speaking, gazing out into the night. Katherine's face was swollen and bruised, and she methodically bathed her injured eye with a cloth which she dipped from time to time into a bowl of warm water before her. They had not uttered a word since the events of the afternoon, but merely shared one another's presence. The fear that passed between them was a fear that other parents had known: the first realization that there was something wrong with their child. It crystallized in silence, but it was not real unless voiced.

Katherine tested the bowl of water with her hand, and, finding it cold, she wrung the cloth out, pushing it away. The movement caused Thorn to gaze at her, and he waited until she was aware of it.

"Sure you don't want to call a doctor?" he asked quietly.

She shook her head.

"Just a few scratches."

"I mean . . . for Damien," said Thorn.

All she could offer was a helpless shrug.

"What would we tell him?" she whispered.

"We don't have to tell him anything. Just . . . have him examine him."

"He had a checkup just last month. There's nothing wrong with him. He's never been sick a day in his life."

Thorn nodded, pondering it.

"He never has, has he?" he remarked curiously.

"No."

"That's strange, isn't it?"

"Is it?"

"I think so."

His tone was odd and she turned to look at him. Their eyes held, Katherine waiting for him to continue.

"I mean . . . no measles or mumps . . . or chicken-pox. Not even a runny nose or a cough. Or a cold."

"So?" she asked defensively.

"I just . . . think it's unusual."

"I don't."

"I do."

"He comes from healthy stock."

Thorn was stopped, and a knot within him tightened. The secret was still there. Down in the pit of his stomach. It had never left him, in all these years, but mostly, he had felt justified about it; guilty for the deception, but soothed by all the happiness it had brought. When things were going well, it was easy to hold it down, keep it dormant. But now it was some-how becoming important, and he felt it burgeoning in him as though it would clog his throat.

"If your family or mine," continued Katherine, "had a history of . . . psychosis, mental disorder . . . then frankly I'd worry about what happened today."

He looked at her, then averted his eyes.

"But I've been thinking about it," she continued, "and I know it's all right. He's a fine, healthy boy. Healthy ancestry right up and down both our family trees."

Unable to look at her, Thorn slowly nodded.

"He had a fright, that's all," added Katherine. "Just a . . . bad moment. Surely every child is entitled to that."

Thorn nodded again, and, with great fatigue, rubbed his forehead. Inside he longed to tell her, have it out in the open. But it was too late. The deception had gone on too long. She would hate him for it. She might even hate the child. It was too late. She must never know.

"I've been thinking about Mrs. Baylock," said Katherine.

"Yes?"

"I've been thinking we should keep her."

"She seemed very nice today," said Thorn quietly.

"Damien is having anxieties. Maybe because he heard us talking about her in the car."

"Yes," replied Thorn.

It made sense. It could have caused the fear in the car. They thought he wasn't listening, but obviously he was taking it all in. The thought of losing her had filled him with terror.

"Yes," Thorn said again, and his voice was filled with hope.

"I'd like to give her other duties," said Katherine. "So she'll be away from home for a while in the day. Maybe have her do the afternoon shopping so I can start spending more time with Daimen."

"Who does it now? The shopping."

"Mrs. Horton."

"Will she mind giving it up?"

"I don't know. But I want to spend more time with Damien."

"I think that's wise."

They fell silent again, and Katherine turned away.

"I think that's good," reiterated Thorn. "I think that's wise."

For an instant he felt that everything was going to be all right. And then he saw that Katherine was crying. It tore at him, and he watched, helpless to comfort her.

"You were right, Kathy," he whispered. "Damien heard us talking about firing her. That's all it was. It was as simple as that."

"I pray," she responded in a quivering voice.

"Of course . . ." he whispered. "That's all it was."

She nodded, and when the tears had subsided, she stood, looking up at the darkened house.

"Well," she said, "the best thing to do with a bad day is to end it. I'm going up to bed."

"I'll just sit out here for a while. I'll be up in a minute."

Her footsteps faded behind him, leaving him alone with his thoughts.

As he gazed out into the forest, he saw instead the hospital in Rome; saw himself there, standing before a window, agreeing to take the child. Why had he not asked more about the mother? Who was she? Where had she come from? Who was the father, and why was he not there? Over the years he had made certain assumptions and they had served to calm his fears. Damien's real mother was probably a peasant girl, a girl of the Church, therefore delivering her child in a Catholic hospital. It was an expensive hospital and she wouldn't have been there without that kind of connection. She was probably an orphan herself, thus no family, and the child was born out of wedlock, this the reason no father was on hand. What else was there to know? What else could have mattered? The child was beautiful and alert, described as "perfect in every way."

Thorn was unaccustomed to doubting himself, to accusing himself; his mind struggled for reassurance that what he had done was right. He had been confused and desperate at the time. He had been vulnerable, an easy prey to suggestion. Could it possibly have been wrong? Could there have been more he needed to know?

The answers to those questions would never be known to Thorn. Only a handful of people knew them and by now they were scattered across the globe. There was Sister Teresa, Father Spilletto, and Father Tassone. Only they knew. It was for their consciences alone. In darkness of that long-distant night they had worked in feverish silence, in the tension and honor of having been chosen. In all of earth's history it had been attempted just twice before, and they knew that, this time, it must not fail. It was all in their hands, just the three of them, and it had moved like clockwork, and no one had known. After the birth, it was Sister Teresa who prepared the impostor, depilitating his arms and forehead, powdering him dry so he would look presentable when Thorn was brought up to view. The hair on his head was thick, as they had hoped, and she used a hairdryer to fluff it, first checking the scalp to make sure the birthmark was there. Thorn would never see Sister Teresa, nor would he see the diminutive Father Tassone who was at work in the basement crating two bodies to be immediately shipped away. The first body was that of Thorn's child, silenced before it uttered its first cry; the second was that of the animal, the surrogate mother of the one who survived. Outside, a truck was waiting to carry the bodies to Cerveteri, where in the silence of Cimitero di Sant' Angelo, gravediggers waited beneath the shrine.

The plan had been born of diabolical communion, and Spilletto was in charge, having chosen his accomplices with the utmost care. He was satisfied with Sister Teresa, but in the final moments became concerned about Tassone. The diminutive scholar was devout, but his belief was born of fear, and on the last day he demonstrated an instability that gave Spilletto pause. Tassone was eager, but his eagerness was self-oriented, a desperation to prove he was worthy of the job. He had lost sight of the significance of what they were doing, preoccupied instead with the importance of his own role. The self-consciousness led to anxiety, and Spilletto came close to dismissing Tassone. If one of them failed, all three would be held responsible. And more important, it could not be attempted again for another thousand years.

In the end, Tassone proved himself, performing his job with dedication and dispatch, even handling a crisis that none of them anticipated. The child was not yet dead and made a sound within his crate as it was being put onto the truck. Quickly removing the crate, Tassone returned with it to the hospital basement and himself made certain that no cry would ever come again. It had shaken him. Deeply. But he had done it, and that was all that mattered.

Around them that night in the hospital, all things appeared to be normal; doctors and nurses carrying on their routine without the slightest knowledge of what was happening in their midst. It had been performed with discretion and exactitude, and no one, especially not Thorn, had ever had a clue.

As he sat now on his patio, gazing out into the night, Thorn realized that the Pereford forest no longer was foreboding to him. He did not have the feeling, as before, that there was something watching him from within. It was peaceful now, the crickets and frogs creating their din. And it was relaxing, somehow reassuring, that life around him was normal. His eyes shifted toward the house, traveling upward to Damien's window. It was illuminated by a nightlight, and Thorn speculated on the child's face in the peacefulness of sleep. It would be the right vision to end this frightening day with, and he rose, switching off a lamp and moving into the darkened house.

It was pitch black inside and the air seemed to ring with silence. Thorn felt his way toward the stairs. There, he groped for a lightswitch, and finding none, proceeded silently upward, until he had reached the landing. He had never seen the house this dark, and realized he must have been outside, lost in thought, for a considerable time. Around him, he could hear the sound of slumbered breathing, and he walked quietly, feeling his way along the wall. His hand hit a lightswitch and he flicked it, but it did not work; he continued on, turning a bend in the long, angular hall. Ahead he could see Damien's room, a faint shaft of light coming from under the door. But he suddenly froze, for he thought he heard a sound. It was a kind of vibration, a low rumble, gone before he could identify it, replaced only by the silent atmosphere of the hall. He prepared to step forward, but the sound came again, louder this time, causing his heart to start pounding. Then he looked down and saw the eyes. With a sudden gasp, he flattened himself against the wall, the growl rising in intensity as a dog materialized from the darkness and stood guard before the child's door. With his breath coming shallow, Thorn stood petrified, the gutteral sound rising, the eyes glaring back.

"Whoa ... whoa ..." uttered Thorn on a shaking breath, and his voice caused the animal to coil tighter, as if ready to spring.

"Quiet down, now," said Mrs. Baylock as she appeared from her room. "This is the master of the house."

And the dog fell silent, the drama suddenly ended. Mrs. Baylock touched a lightswitch and the hall was instantly illuminated, leaving Thorn breathless, staring down at the dog.

"What ... is this?" he gasped.

"Sir?" asked Mrs. Baylock casually.

"This dog."

"Shepherd, I think. Isn't he beautiful? We found him in the forest."

The dog lay at her feet now, suddenly unconcerned.

"Who gave you permission ... ?"

"I thought we could use a good watchdog, and the boy absolutely loves him."

Thorn was still shaken, standing stiffly against the wall, and Mrs. Baylock could not hide her amusement.

"Gave you a fright, did he?"

"Yes."

"See how good he is? As a watchdog, I mean? Believe me, you'll be grateful to have him here when you're gone."

"When I'm gone?" asked Thorn.

"On your trip. Aren't you going to Saudi Arabia?"

"How do you know about Saudi Arabia?" he asked.

She shrugged. "I didn't know it was a secret."

"I haven't told anybody here."

"It was Mrs. Horton told me."

Thorn nodded, his eyes moving again toward the dog.

"He won't be any trouble," assured the woman. "We're only going to feed him scraps . . ."

"I don't want him here," snapped Thorn.

She gazed at him with surprise. "You don't like dogs?"

"When I want a dog, I'll choose it."

"The boy's taken quite a fancy to it, sir, and I think he needs it."

"I'll decide when he needs a dog."

"Children can count on animals, sir. No matter what."

She gazed at him as though there was something else she was trying to convey.

"Are you . . . trying to tell me something?"

"I wouldn't presume to, sir."

But the way she looked at him made it plain.

"If you have something to say, Mrs. Baylock, I'd like to hear it."

"I shouldn't, sir. You've enough on your mind . . ."

"I said I'd like to hear it."

"Just that the child seems lonely."

"Why should he be lonely?"

"His mother doesn't seem to accept him."

Thorn stiffened, affronted by the remark.

"You see?" she said, "I shouldn't have spoken."

"Doesn't accept him?"

"She doesn't seem to like him. And he feels it, too."

Thorn was speechless, not knowing what to say.

"Sometimes I think all he has is me," the woman added.

"I think you're mistaken."

"And now he has this dog. He loves this dog. For his sake, don't take it away."

Thorn gazed down at the massive animal and shook his head. "I don't like this dog," he said. "Tomorrow take him to the pound."

"The pound?" she gasped.

"The Humane Society."

"They *kill* them there!"

"Just get him out, then. Tomorrow I want him gone."

Mrs. Baylock's face hardened and Thorn turned away. The woman and the dog watched him move away down the long hall, and their eyes burned with hatred.

Chapter Five

Thorn had spent a sleepless night. He sat on the bedroom terrace smoking cigarettes, disgusted by their taste. From the room behind him he heard Katherine moan, and he wondered what demon she fought in her sleep. Was it the old one, the demon of depression come back to haunt? Or was she simply replaying the awful events of the day?

To keep his mind off reality, he began to speculate, retreating into his imagination to drive off immediate concerns. He thought about dreams, the possibility of one man's seeing another's. Brain activity was known to be electrical; so were the impulses that created images on television screens. Surely there was a way to carry one to the other. Imagine the therapeutic good it could do. The dreams could even be put on video tape so the dreamer could replay them in detail. He himself had often been haunted by a vague sensation that he had had a troubling dream. But by morning the details were lost, leaving only the feeling of uneasiness. Besides being therapeutic, think how entertaining such taped dreams could be. And how dangerous, too. The dreams of great men could be stored in archives for future generations to see. What were Napoleon's dreams? Or Hitler's? Or Lee Harvey Oswald's? Maybe Kennedy's assassination could have been averted if someone could have seen Oswald's dreams. Surely there must be a way. And in this manner Thorn passed the hours until morning.

When Katherine awoke, her injured eye was swollen shut, and as Thorn left he suggested she see a doctor.

It was the only conversation they exchanged. Katherine was silent, and Thorn was preoccupied with the day that lay ahead. He was to make final arrangements for his trip to Saudi Arabia, but he had the feeling that he should not go. He was afraid. For Katherine, for Damien, and for himself; yet he didn't know why. There was uncertainty in the air, a feeling that life was suddenly fragile. He had never before been preoccupied with a sense of death, it was always far away. But *that* was the essence of what he was feeling now. That his life was somehow in danger.

In the limousine on the way to the Embassy, he made perfunctory notes about insurance policies and business details that would have to be attended to in the event of his death. He did it dispassionately and without the realization that it was something he had never done, or even considered doing, before. Only when he was finished did the act frighten him, and he sat in tense silence as the car approached the Embassy, feeling that at any moment something was going to happen.

As the limousine came to a stop, Thorn moved stiffly out, waiting there until it had pulled away. And then he saw them descending on him; two men moving fast, one taking pictures, the other firing questions. Thorn headed toward the Embassy, but they got in his way; he tried to step around them, shaking his head in response to their questions.

"Have you read today's *Reporter*, Mr. Thorn?"

"No, I haven't . . ."

"There's an article about your nanny, the one that jumped . . ."

"I didn't see it."

"It says she left a suicide note."

"Nonsense."

"Could you look this way, please?" It was Jennings with the camera, moving quickly, clicking away.

56

"Would you mind?" asked Thorn as Jennings blocked his way.

"Is it true she was involved with drugs?" asked the other.

"Of course not."

"The coroner's report said there was a drug in her bloodstream."

"It was an allergy drug," replied Thorn through clenched teeth. "She had allergies . . ."

"They said it was an overdose."

"Could you hold it like that?" asked Jennings.

"Would you get out of my way?" Thorn growled.

"Just doing my job, sir."

Thorn sidestepped, but they pursued him once again, getting in his way.

"Did she use drugs, Mr. Thorn?"

"I told you . . ."

"The article said . . ."

"I don't care what the article said!"

"That's great!" said Jennings. "Just hold it like that!"

The camera came too close and Thorn pushed it aside, knocking it from Jennings' hand. It crashed hard on the cement, and for a moment everyone stood in silence, shocked by the burst of sudden violence.

"Can't you people have some respect?" Thorn gasped.

Jennings knelt, gazing up at him from his knees.

"I'm sorry," said Thorn in a shaking voice. "Send me a bill for the damage."

Jennings picked up the broken camera and stood slowly, shrugging as he looked into Thorn's eyes.

"That's okay, Mr. Ambassador," he said. "Let's just say . . . you 'owe' me."

After an uneasy nod, Thorn turned on his heel and entered the Embassy, as a Marine ran up from the street, too late to survey the aftermath of the incident.

"He busted my camera," said Jennings to the Marine. "The Ambassador busted my camera."

They stood nonplussed, then disbursed, each going his separate way.

Thorn's office was in turmoil. The trip of Saudi Arabia was in jeopardy because Thorn was balking, saying, without further explanation, that he was unable to go. Planning the trip had occupied his staff for the better part of two weeks, and his two aides were up in arms, feeling cheated that their work had gone to waste.

"You can't cancel," entreated one. "After all this, you can't just call and say . . ."

"It's not canceled," retorted Thorn, "it's postponed."

"They'll take it as an insult."

"So be it."

"But why?"

"I don't feel like traveling right now," replied Thorn. "It's not a good time."

"Do you realize what's at *stake* here?" asked his second aide.

"Diplomacy," answered Thorn.

"More than that."

"They've got the oil and they've got the power," said Thorn. "Nothing will change that."

"That's precisely why . . ."

"I'll send somebody else."

"The President's expecting you to go."

"I'll talk to him. I'll explain."

"My God, Jerry! This thing's been planned for weeks!"

"Then replan it!" Thorn shouted.

His sudden outburst created silence. An intercom buzzed, and Thorn reached for it.

"Yes?"

"There's a Father Tassone here to see you," replied a secretary's voice.

"Who?"

"Father Tassone from Rome. He says it's a matter of urgent personal business."

"I've never heard of him," replied Thorn.

"He says he just needs a minute," responded the voice. "Something about a hospital."

"Probably wants a donation," mumbled one of Thorn's aides.

"Or a dedication," added the other.

"All right," Thorn sighed. "Send him in."

"I didn't know you were such a soft touch," remarked one of the aides.

"Public relations," muttered Thorn.

"Don't make a decision on Saudi Arabia yet. Okay? You're down today. Just let it sit."

"The decision is made," said Thorn with fatigue. "Either someone else goes or we postpone it."

"Postpone it until when?"

"Until later," responded Thorn. "Until I feel better about leaving."

The doors swung open, and in the massive archway stood a diminutive man. He was a priest; his robes were disheveled, his manner tense, his sense of urgency felt by all in the room. The aides exchanged an uneasy glance, uncertain whether it was safe to leave the room.

"Would it . . . be all right . . ." asked the priest, in a thick Italian accent, ". . . to speak with you alone?"

"It's about a hospital?" asked Thorn.

"Si."

After a moment, Thorn nodded, and his aides moved hesitantly from the room. When they were gone, the priest closed the doors behind them; then he turned, his expression filled with pain.

"Yes?" Thorn asked apprehensively.

"We have not much time."

"What?"

"You must listen to what I say."

The priest refused to move, remaining with his back touching the door.

"And what is that?" asked Thorn.

"You must accept Christ as your Saviour. You must accept him now."

And there passed a moment of silence, Thorn at a loss for words.

"Please, signor . . ."

"Excuse me," interrupted Thorn. "Did I understand you to have a matter of urgent personal business?"

"You must take communion," the priest continued. "Drink the blood of Christ and eat his flesh, for only if He is within you can you defeat the child of the Devil."

The atmosphere in the room burned with tension. Thorn's hand reached for the intercom.

"He's killed once," whispered the priest, "and he'll kill again. He'll kill until everything that's yours is his."

"If you'll just wait outside . . ."

The priest had begun to approach now, his voice rising in intensity.

"Only through Christ can you fight him," he entreated. "Accept the Lord Jesus. Drink of His blood."

Thorn's hand found the intercom button and pushed.

"I've locked the door, Mr. Thorn," said the priest.

Thorn stiffened, frightened now by the priest's tone.

"Yes?" asked the secretary's voice through the intercom.

"Send for a security guard," replied Thorn.

"What's that, sir?"

"I beg you, signor," pleaded the priest, "listen to what I say."

"Sir?" repeated the secretary.

"I was at the hospital, Mr. Thorn," said the priest, "the night your son was born."

Thorn was jolted. Riveted in place.

"I . . . was a . . . midwife," the priest said in a faltering voice. "I . . . witnessed . . . the *birth*."

The secretary's voice came again, this time edged with concern.

"Mr. Thorn?" she said. "I'm sorry, I didn't hear you."

"Nothing," responded Thorn. "Just . . . stand by."

He released the button, gazing fearfully back at the priest.

"I beg you . . ." said Tassone, choking back tears.

"What do you want?"

"To save you, Mr. Thorn. So Christ will forgive me."

"What do you know about my son?"

"Everything."

"What do you know?" demanded Thorn.

The priest was trembling now, his voice thick with emotion.

"I saw its mother," he replied.

"You saw my wife?"

"I saw its mother!"

"You're referring to my wife?"

"Its *mother*, Mr. Thorn!"

Thorn's face hardened, and he gazed back evenly at the priest.

"Is this blackmail?" he asked quietly.

"No, sir."

"Then what do you want?"

"To *tell* you, sir."

"To tell me what?"

"Its mother, sir . . ."

"Go on, what *about* her?"

"Its mother, sir . . . was a *jackal*!" A sob escaped the priest's throat. "He was born of a *jackal*! I saw it myself!"

With a sudden crash, Thorn's door flew open, a Marine entering, Thorn's aides and secretary behind him. Thorn was ashen, immobile, the priest's face wet with tears.

"Something wrong in here, sir?" asked the Marine.

"You sounded strange," added the secretary. "And the door was locked."

"I want this man escorted out of here," said Thorn. "And if he ever comes back ... I want him put in jail."

No one moved, the Marine hesitant to put his hands on a priest. Slowly, Tassone turned and walked to the door. There he stopped, looking back at Thorn.

"Accept Christ," he whispered sadly. "Each day drink His blood."

Then he left, the Marine following him, all the others standing in confused silence.

"What did he want?" an aide asked.

"I don't know," whispered Thorn gazing after the priest. "He was crazy."

On the street outside the Embassy, Haber Jennings leaned up against a car, checking out his spare camera, having put the broken one away. His eye caught sight of the Marine escorting the priest down the front steps, and he snapped off a couple of shots of the two as the priest slowly shuffled away. The Marine spotted Jennings and walked to him, eyeing him with distaste.

"Haven't you gotten into enough trouble with that thing today?" he asked, indicating Jennings' camera.

"Enough *trouble*?" smiled Jennings. "*Never* enough."

And he clicked off two more shots of the Marine at point-blank range, the Marine glaring as he withdrew. Then Jennings changed focus and found the small priest; he snapped off one more shot of him as he disappeared in the distance.

Late that night, Jennings sat in his darkroom gazing at a series of photographs, his eyes curious and confused. To make sure his spare camera was operating efficiently he had shot off a roll of thirty-six pictures at varying exposures and speeds, and three of them had turned out defective. It was the same sort of defect he'd had a few months ago in the shot of the nanny at the Thorn estate. This time it involved the shots of the priest. Once again it seemed to be a flaw on the emulsion, but this time it appeared more than once. It came twice in a row, then skipped two shots, then returned, exactly as before. Even more curious, it seemed linked to the subject, the strange blur of movement hanging above the priest's head as though it were somehow actually there.

Jennings lifted five photos from the developer and examined them closely under the light: two shots of the priest with the Marine, two close-ups of the Marine alone, then one more of the priest alone in the distance. Not only did the blemish disappear in the two shots of the Marine, but when it reappeared in the final shot, it was smaller in size, relative to the size of the priest. As before it was a kind of a halo, but *unlike* the blemish that defaced the photo of the nanny, this one was oblong in shape, suspended well over the subject's head. The haze that enveloped the head of the nanny was inert, conveying a sense of peace, but the one above the priest's head was dynamic, as though in motion. It looked like a ghostlike javelin about to skewer the priest to the ground.

Jennings reached for an opium joint and sat back to speculate. He had read once that film emulsion was sensitive to extreme heat, just as it was to light. The article appeared in a photographic journal and dealt with ghostlike images that showed up on film taken in one of England's famed haunted houses. The writer, an expert in photographic science, had speculated on the relationship of nitrate to temperature change, noting that in laboratory experiments intense heat had been found to affect film emulsion the same way as light. Heat was energy, and energy was heat, and if indeed, apparitions were, as some speculated, residual human energy, then under the right circumstances their shape could be recorded on film. But the energy the article spoke of was without relation to the human body. What was the meaning of energy that clung to the outside of a human form? Did it come at random, or did it have some *meaning*? Did it have to do with external influences, or was it perhaps born of anxieties festering within?

Anxiety was known to create energy, this the principle of the polygraph used for lie detector tests. *That* energy was electrical in nature. Electricity was also heat. Perhaps the heat generated by extreme anxiety burst through human flesh and could thus be photographed surrounding people in states of great stress.

All this excited Jennings, and he dug through his film emulsion charts, finding the order number of the most light-sensitive film made—Tri-X-600, a new product so sensitive that one could photograph fast action by candlelight. It was probably the most heat-sensitive as well.

The next morning, Jennings bought twenty-four rolls of Tri-X-600 and a series of accompanying filters to experiment with the film outdoors. The filters would cut out light, but possibly not heat, and he would have a better chance of finding what he was looking for. He needed to find subjects in states of extreme stress, and so he went to a hospital, there secretly photographing patients in the terminal ward who knew they were dying. The results were disappointing, for in ten rolls taken, not a single blemish appeared. Clearly, whatever the blemishes were, they had nothing to do with an awareness of death.

Jennings was frustrated but undismayed, for he knew instinctively he was on to something. Returning to his darkroom, he redeveloped the photos of the priest and the nanny, experimenting with different textures of paper, blowing them up to closely examine every grain. It was plain, in enlargement, that something was actually there. The naked eye had not seen it, but the nitrate had responded. Indeed, there were invisible images in the air.

All this occupied his time and thoughts for a solid week. And then he reemerged to once again follow Thorn.

The Ambassador had embarked on a series of speaking engagements, and it was easy for Jennings to get access. He appeared at local university campuses, business luncheons, even a factory or two, and was on display for all to see. The Ambassador's style was eloquent, filled with fervor, and he seemed to win his audiences wherever he went. If this was his forte, it was the most valuable asset a political hopeful could have. He stirred people, and they believed in him, particularly the working class, the economic underdogs, for the Ambassador seemed genuinely concerned.

"We stand divided in so many ways!" they would hear him shout. "Old and young, rich and poor . . . but most important, those who have a chance, and those who do *not*! Democracy is equal opportunity. And without equal opportunity the word 'democracy' is a lie!"

He made himself available to the public on these speaking tours, often making special efforts to make contact with handicapped people he would spot in the crowd. He seemed the image of a champion, and more important even than his own innate abilities was the fact that he could make people *believe*.

In truth, however, the very fervor that people responded to was born of desperation. Thorn was running, using his public duties to avoid personal distress, for a growing sense of foreboding followed him wherever he went. Twice, in the crowds that gathered to hear him speak, he had spotted a familiar clerical black outfit, and he began to feel that the small priest was stalking him. He avoided telling anyone, because he feared it was his own imagination, but he began to become preoccupied with it, searching the crowds as he spoke to them, fearing the appearance of the priest wherever he went. He had dismissed Tassone's words; plainly the man was insane, a religious zealot obsessed with a public figure, and the fact that his obsession involved Thorn's child could be nothing more than coincidence. And yet the priest's words haunted him. Impossible as they were, they echoed in Thorn's mind, and he fought continually against giving them weight. It occurred to Thorn that the priest might be a potential assassin, for in the cases of both Lee Harvey Oswald and Arthur Bremmer, the assassins tried to make personal contact of the kind the priest had made. But he dismissed this as well. He could no longer move as he had to if he dwelt on the spectre of death waiting in the crowds. And yet the priest stayed with him; in his waking hours and in his sleep, until Thorn became aware he was as obsessed with the man as the man was with him. Tassone was the predator, Thorn the prey. He felt as a fieldmouse must feel, fearing always, that high above, he was being circled by a hawk.

At Pereford the surface was calm. But in the depths of hidden feelings the fires of anxiety burned bright. Thorn and Katherine saw little of each other, his speaking engagements and other duties keeping him away. When they came together, they kept their conversation on a surface level, avoiding anything that would cause distress. Katherine was spending more time with Damien, as she had promised, but it only served to accentuate their distance, the child whiling away the hours in silence, enduring the time rather than enjoying it, until Mrs. Baylock returned.

With his nanny, he was able to laugh and play, but with Katherine he was withdrawn; in frustration she attempted, day after day, to find ways of bringing him out of his shell. She bought coloring books and paint sets, building blocks and wheeled toys, but always they were met with the same dulled response. One afternoon he evidenced interest in an animal cut-out book, and it was then that she decided to take him to the zoo.

As she packed her station wagon for a day's outing, it occurred to her how different their lives were from those of normal people. Her child was four and a half years old and he had never even been to a zoo. As the Ambassador's family, everything was brought to them, they rarely sought things out. Perhaps it was this lack of normal childhood adventures that had dulled Damien's sense of fun. But today there was life in his eyes, and as he sat beside her in the car, she could sense she had finally done something right. He even talked. Not much, but more than usual—struggling with the word "hippopotamus," and giggling when he finally got it right. How little it took to make Katherine happy; a giggle from her child caused her spirits to soar. As they headed for the city, she talked nonstop, and Damien listened intently. Lions were just big cats and gorillas were just big monkeys, and squirrels were related to rats, and horses related to donkeys. He was delighted, absorbing it all, and Katherine made a poem of it, repeating it as they drove. Lions are cats and gorillas monkeys, and squirrels are rats and horses are donkeys. She said it fast and Damien laughed, and she said it faster and he laughed harder. It convulsed him, and they laughed together all the way to the zoo.

On a bright Sunday in winter everyone in London tries to get outdoors; people were everywhere, greedily soaking up fresh air and sun. It was an uncommonly beautiful day and the zoo was packed to capacity. The animals also seemed to be enjoying the sun, their growls and howls heard all the way to the admission gate where Katherine rented a stroller so she could push Damien and not have their day hampered by fatigue.

They stopped first at the swans and watched the beautiful creatures flock around a group of children

67

who were feeding them bread. They pushed through to get a front-row vantage, but at that moment the swans suddenly became disinterested in feeding and majestically turned their tails, slowly paddling away, In midpond they stopped, gazing back like disdainful monarchs, the children pleading and throwing bread. But the swans would not return to feed, Katherine noticing that only after she and Damien left did their hunger appear to have once again returned.

It was near lunchtime and the crowds were thickening; Katherine searched for any cage or exhibit that wasn't surrounded by people. Off to the right was a sign marked PRAIRIE DOGS and she headed toward it, telling Damien everything she knew about prairie dogs on the way. They lived in burrows in the desert, she said, and were very sociable; people in America often captured them and raised them as pets. As they neared the exhibit Katherine found that it too was surrounded by people, all gazing down into a pit. She pushed her way through but saw the animals for no more than an instant, for, in a sudden explosive movement, they all disappeared into their dens. The crowd around her mumbled with disappointment and began to disperse. When Damien craned his neck to see, all there was was a mound of dirt riddled with holes, and he gazed at his mother with dismay.

"Must be lunchtime for them, too," she shrugged.

They pushed on, stopping for hotdogs, eating them as they sat on a bench.

"We'll go see the monkeys," said Katherine. "Would you like to see the monkeys?"

The path to the Monkey House was clearly marked with signs; following them, they approached a line of cages, Damien's eyes lighting with excitement as the first animal came into view. It was a bear, pacing mechanically back and forth in its confines, oblivious to the people gawking from the other side of the bars. But as Katherine and Damien came near, the bear seemed to notice them. It stopped and glared, its back bristling as they slowly moved by. In the adjoining cage was a large cat, and it too ceased to move; its yellowed eyes riveted upon them, following them as they passed. Next was a baboon, which suddenly bared its teeth, clearly singling them out from the many others who passed. Katherine began to sense the effect they were having on the animals, and she watched them carefully as she passed cage after cage. It was Damien they were watching. And he seemed to feel it too.

"Guess they think you look pretty delicious," smiled Katherine. "I think you do, too."

And she steered him away from the cages, taking another path. Whoops and chattering could be heard resounding from a building ahead, and Katherine knew they were close to the monkeys. It was the most popular of all the indoor exhibits, and they had to wait in line, Katherine parking the stroller and carrying Damien in her arms.

Inside, the atmosphere was hot and fetid; the din of children's squeals echoed off the walls, the sound somehow amplified by the confinement. From their position by the door they could see nothing, but Katherine sensed, by the people's reaction, that the monkeys were performing in a far cage. With Damien in her arms, she pushed into the mob, forcing her way until they got a glimpse of what was happening. It was a cage of spider monkeys and they were in high gear, swinging on tires and bounding in all directions, pleasing the crowd with their acrobatics. Damien was excited, beginning to laugh, and Katherine pushed forcefully ahead, determined to get him a front-row view. The monkeys were oblivious to their audience, but as Katherine and Damien came forward, the mood within the cage seemed to change. The playful activity stopped as, one by one, the animals began to turn, their small eyes darting nervously, searching the crowd. The crowd too fell silent, curious that the animals had stopped, but waiting with anticipatory smiles for the action to suddenly resume. When it did, it was in a way that no one expected. There was a sudden howl within the cage, a shriek of fear or warning, and as it rose, all the animals joined in. In a desperate surge, the cage exploded with movement, the monkeys bounding frantically about their cage, trying to get out. Cramming toward the rear of the cage, they strained to break the wire-mesh window; panicked, as though a predator had suddenly been let loose in their midst. In their frenzy, they clawed at one another, blood beginning to flow as their paws and teeth sought desperately for escape. The crowd stood silent, aghast, but Damien was laughing, pointing at the horrifying scene and squealing with delight. Within the cage, the panic rose, a large monkey propelling himself upward through a wire-mesh ceiling, caught there by the neck, his body jerking until it went limp. People cried out in horror, some heading for the doors, but their cries were drowned out by the wail of the animals, wild-eyed and salivating now, propelled by sheer terror as they bounded from wall to wall. One among them began hurling its body headlong into the solid concrete, blood covering its face until it staggered and fell, its body convulsing as others jumped around it and shrieked in horror. There was pushing now in the crowd of onlookers, the people themselves panicking as they desperately sought to escape. Despite being shoved and jostled, Katherine was somehow frozen in place. Her child was laughing. Pointing and laughing, as though somehow promoting the suicidal din. It was *he* they were frightened of. *He* who was doing it. And as the holocaust increased, Katherine began to scream.

Chapter Six

Katherine returned home late that night, Damien already asleep in the car. After the zoo they had merely driven, the child sitting in silence, hurt and confused as to what was wrong. He tried to repeat the poem once, the one about gorillas and monkeys and horses and donkeys, but Katherine was mute, her gaze fixed firmly ahead. When darkness came, Damien indicated he was hungry, but his mother refused to respond, and he crawled into the back seat, where he found a blanket, and fell asleep.

Katherine drove swiftly but aimlessly, trying to escape the fear that was overtaking her. It was not the fear of Damien, or of Mrs. Baylock. It was the fear that she was going insane.

At Pereford, Jeremy was waiting, expecting to find her in good spirits; he had asked that dinner be held until she arrived. They sat now at a small table, Thorn's eyes on Katherine as she quietly, and tensely tried to eat.

"Are you all right, Katherine?"

"Yes."

"So silent."

"Just tired, I guess."

"Full day?"

"Yes."

Her manner was abrupt, as though she resented the intrusion.

"Was it fun?"

"Yes."

"You seem disturbed."

"Do I?"

"What's wrong?"

"What could be wrong?"

"I don't know. You seem upset."

"Just tired. I just need some sleep."

She feigned a smile, but it was not convincing. Thorn was troubled as he studied her.

"Damien all right?" asked Thorn.

"Yes."

"Are you sure?"

"Yes."

Thorn watched her, and she averted her eyes.

"If there were anything 'wrong' . . . you'd tell me, wouldn't you?" he asked. "I mean . . . with Damien?"

"With Damien? What could be wrong with Damien, Jeremy? What could be wrong with our son? We are the 'blessed' people, aren't we?"

She caught his eye and seemed to smile, but the expression showed no pleasure.

"I mean, only 'goodness' comes to the House of the Thorns," she said. "Black clouds just stay away."

"There *is* something wrong, isn't there?" asked Thorn quietly.

Katherine lowered her head into her hands and remained immobile.

"Kathy . . ." said Thorn gently. "What *is* it?"

"I think . . ." she replied, struggling to control her voice, ". . . I want to see a doctor." She raised her eyes, and they were filled with pain. "I have . . . 'fears,'" she said. "Fears that a normal person wouldn't have."

"Kathy . . ." Thorn whispered. "What kind of fears?"

"If I told you, you'd have me locked up."

"No . . ." he assured her. "No . . . I love you."

"Then help me," she pleaded. "Find me a doctor."

A tear had slid from her eye, and Thorn reached for her hands.

"Of course," he said. "Of course."

And she wept, the events of the day remaining locked, forever, inside her.

Psychiatrists were not as common in England as they were in America, and it was with some difficulty that Thorn found one he felt he could trust. He was American, younger than Thorn would have preferred, but well recommended, with a broad range of experience. His name was Charles Greer. Schooled at Princeton, interned at Bellevue, he was of particular interest because he had lived for a time in Georgetown and had treated several senators' wives.

"The common problem among politicians' wives is alcoholism," said Greer as Thorn sat before him in the psychiatrist's office. "I think it's the feeling of isolation. The feeling of inadequacy. The fear that they have no identity of their own."

"You understand the need for confidence," said Thorn.

"That's all I have to sell," smiled the psychiatrist. "People confide in me, and frankly that's all I have to offer. They don't discuss their problems with other people precisely because they think their confidences will come back to haunt them. I'm safe. I can't promise much, but I can promise you that."

"Shall I have her call you?"

"Just give her my number. Don't *have* her call."

"It's not that she doesn't want to. She asked me . . ."

"Good."

As Thorn rose uneasily, the young doctor smiled.

"Will you call me after you've seen her?" asked Thorn.

"I doubt it," Greer replied simply.

"I mean . . . if you have something to say?"

"What I have to say I'll say to *her*."

"I mean, if you're *worried* about her . . ."

"Is she suicidal?"

". . . No."

"Then I won't be worried about her. I'm sure it's not as serious as you think."

Reassured, Thorn headed for the door.

"Mr. Thorn?"

"Yes?"

"Why did you come here today?"

"To see you."

"For what reason?"

Thorn shrugged. "See what you looked like, I guess."

"Was there something in particular you wanted to say?"

Thorn was uneasy. After pondering he shook his head.

"Are you suggesting that *I* might want to see a psychiatrist?"

"Do you?"

"Do I look like I need one?"

"Do I?" asked the psychiatrist.

"No."

"Well, I have one," smiled Greer. "In my line of work I'd be in trouble if I didn't."

The conversation was unsettling, and after Thorn returned to his office, he mused upon it all day. When with Greer, he had felt an urge to talk, to tell him things he had told no one before. But what good would it do? The deception was something he had to live with, a fact of life. And yet he longed for someone else to know.

The day passed slowly, as Thorn attempted to prepare an important speech. It was to be delivered the following evening to a group of prominent businessmen, and it was likely that representatives of Arab oil interests would be there. Thorn wanted it to be a special speech, a plea for pacifism. It was the continuing conflict over Israel that was causing the widening rift between the United States and the Arab bloc, and

74

Thorn knew the Arab-Israeli hostilities were historical in nature, deeply rooted in the scriptures. For this reason he looked to the Bible, not one but three, seeking to amplify his understanding with the wisdom of the ages. In truth, there was a more practical reason, for there was not an audience in the world that failed to be impressed with quotations from the scriptures.

He sealed himself off for the afternoon, ordering his lunch in as he studied, and then, finding difficulty locating meaningful passages, he sent a messenger out for a bibliography and interpretive text. It was easier after that, for he could turn to the relevant passages and then, in many cases, find a theological view of their meaning.

It was the first time Thorn had cracked the pages of a Bible since he was a child. He found it fascinating, particularly in the light of the ceaseless violence in the Middle East. He discovered it was the Jew Abraham who was first promised by God that his people would inherit the Holy Land.

> I will multiply thee and I will make of thee a multitude of people. I will give this country to thy posterity and after thee in order that they shall possess it forever.

The country given by God to the Jews was clearly delineated in the Books of Genesis and Joshua as the land extending from the River of Egypt to Lebanon and the Euphrates. Thorn looked at his atlas and found that the State of Israel presently occupied only the narrow strip between Jordan and the Mediterranean. Just a small piece of what God had apparently promised. Could it be that Israel's drive for expansion was dictated by this? Thorn's interest deepened and he looked further. If God could make such a promise, why then could God not fulfill it?

If you keep my covenant you will be for me a
kingdom of priests and a Holy Nation.

Perhaps that was the clue. The Jews had not kept
the Lord's covenant. It was believed, then, that the
Jews had killed Christ. The Book of Deuteronomy
bore this out, for after the death of Christ it was declared to the Jews:

The Lord shall scatter you among the peoples,
and you shall be left few in number among the
Nations where the Lord drives you. You will be
taken captive among all Nations, and Jerusalem
will be trampled under foot by the Gentiles until
the time of the Gentiles be fulfilled.

This was reiterated by the Book of Luke, the word
"Gentiles" replaced with the word "Nations." You will
be trampled under foot until the time of the Nations be
fulfilled. This clearly prophesied that the Jews would
be persecuted throughout history, and then the persecution would stop. But what was the time of the Nations? The time when the persecution would end?

Turning to his interpretive texts, Thorn found evidence of God's wrath. It was an historical log of persecution that began with the Jews being driven from
Israel by King Solomon, then slaughtered by the
Crusaders as they fled. In the year 1000 it had been
documented that twelve thousand Jews were murdered,
then in the year 1200 all who had sought refuge in England were expelled or hanged. In the year 1298 one
hundred thousand Jews were slaughtered in Franconia,
Bavaria, and Austria; in September, 1306, another one
hundred thousand were expelled from France under
threat of death. In 1348 the Jews were accused of having caused a worldwide epidemic of Black Plague, and
more than a million of them were sought out and killed
across the globe. In August, 1492, the very time that

76

Columbus was gaining glory for his country by discovering the New World, the Spanish Inquisition drove out half a million Jews and put another half million to death. The grim log continued, to the time of Hitler who annihilated over six million Jews, leaving only eleven million, homeless and poverty-stricken, across the entire face of the globe. Was it any wonder, the zeal with which they now fought for their refuge, for a country they could call their own? And was it any wonder that they waged each offensive as though it were their last?

> I will make of thee a great Nation, God had promised: And I will bless thee and I will make thy name great; so be thou a blessing . . . and all the families of the earth blessed in Thee.

Thorn turned again to his interpretive texts and found that in God's promise to Abraham were three separate and equally important factors. The gift of a country, Israel. The assurance that Abraham and his descendants would become a great nation. And finally, above all, the "blessing"; the coming of the Saviour. The Jews' return to Zion was linked to the second coming of Christ, and if that were true, the time was now at hand. There was no evidence as to how or when this coming would occur; the prophecies were shrouded in legend and religious symbols. Could Christ already be on earth? Was he again born of woman, and walking among us now?

An instinctive speculator, Thorn's mind roamed the possibilities. If Christ were born on the earth now, he would, as before, be dressed in attire of the day. No more robes and crowns of thorn, but chinos perhaps, or Levis, or a suit and tie. Was he born yet? And if so, why was he silent? Surely the world was in a big enough mess.

Thorn carried these thoughts home and brought his

books as well. After Katherine had retired and the house was dark and silent around him, he opened the books in his study and began to ponder again. It was the return of Christ that sparked his imagination, and he sought out pertinent passages of text. He found it immensely complicated, for it was prophesied in the Book of Revelations that when Christ returned to earth he would have to face his *antithesis*. The Anti-Christ. The Son of Evil. And the earth would be swept asunder by the final contest between Heaven and Hell. It would be Armageddon. The Apocalypse. The end of the world.

From the silence of his den, Thorn heard a sound coming from the upstairs of the house. It was a moan. It came twice and then stopped. Leaving the den, he moved quietly up the stairs and gazed in at Katherine. She was asleep, but restless, her face bathed in sweat. He watched her until her tossing ceased and her breath became even, and then he withdrew, heading back to the stairs. As he felt his way down the darkened hall, he passed Mrs. Baylock's room, noticing the door slightly ajar. The massive woman was asleep on her back, a mountain of flesh spotlighted by the moonlight flooding in through her window. Thorn was about to continue but was suddenly halted, shocked by the woman's face. It was powdered a ghastly white. She was wearing lipstick, too, garishly applied, as though put on in a state of drunken stupor. It was a chilling sight and he felt weakened by it, struggling to sort it out. It made no sense. In the privacy of her room, the woman had painted herself like a harlot.

Closing her door, he returned downstairs, gazing again at the books laid out before him. He was troubled now, unable to concentrate, his eyes idly wandering across the opened pages. The small King James Bible was opened to the Book of Daniel, and he stared at it in silence.

. . . And then shall arise a contemptible one
whom royal majesty has not been given. He shall
come by counterfeit means and obtain the Kingdom by flatteries. Armies shall be swept away before him and broken . . . and he shall act deceit-
fully and he shall become strong with a small
people. Without warning he shall come into the
richest parts; and he shall do what neither his fathers nor his fathers' fathers have done, scattering
among the people plunder, spoils, and goods. He
shall devise plans against strongholds, he shall ex-
alt himself and magnify himself above every God,
and shall speak astonishing things against the God
of Gods. He shall prosper until the indignation is
accomplished, for what is determined shall be
done.

Thorn rummaged through his desk and found a cigarette, then poured himself a glass of wine. He wandered about the room, forcing his mind to deal with his
research, to shut out the uneasiness of what he had
seen upstairs. When the Jews returned to Zion, Christ
was again to be born. And as Christ would be born, so
would the Anti-Christ, both growing separately until
their final confrontation. Thorn stood over his books,
thumbing through them again.

Behold the day of the Lord, a cruel day, a day
of wrath and burning fury which will reduce the
earth to solitude . . . and I shall make men more
rare than fine gold . . . more rare than the gold of
Ophir.

Then, in the Book of Zechariah:

One will seize the hand of the other and they
will lift up their swords against each other. He

will call for a sword against them unto all his mountains, and every man's word will turn against his brother.

Thorn sat down again, gripped by the violence of what the prophecies foretold.

Behold the fury with which the Lord will strike all the peoples who have made war against Jerusalem! Their flesh will fall in rottenness while they are standing on their feet. Their eyes will rot in their sockets and their tongues will rot in their mouths.

Thorn knew the tide of the world was turning against Israel; the Arabs, with their oil, were now too powerful for anyone to stand against. If God's wrath were to turn against the nations that made war on Jerusalem, it was destined to turn against them all. It was prophesied that Armageddon, the final battle, would take place in the arena of the Israelites, with Jesus standing on one side, on the Mount of Olives, the Anti-Christ on the other.

Woe to you, Oh Earth and Sea, for the Devil sends the beast with wrath, because he knows the time is short. . . . Let him who hath understanding reckon the number of the beast, for it is a human number, its number is six hundred and sixty-six.

Armageddon. The end of the world. The battle over Israel.

The Lord will appear . . . his feet shall stand on that day on the Mount of Olives, which is opposite Jerusalem on the eastern side . . . and the Lord God will come and all his holy ones with him.

Thorn closed his books and turned out his desk lamp. He sat for a long time in silence. He wondered what these books were, and who had written them, and why they had been written at all. And he wondered why he believed them, and yet why he rejected them. To believe them made one's efforts futile. Were they all just pawns for the mightier forces of Good and Evil? Were they puppets being manipulated from above and below? Could there really be a Heaven? Could there really be a Hell? He realized these were the questions of an adolescent and yet he could not help but wonder. He had felt it recently, the sensation of powers beyond his control. Not random powers but purposeful ones; sensations that made him feel weak and impermanent. And more than that; *helpless*. That, at the bottom line, was what it all meant. He was helpless. They were all helpless. They didn't ask to be born and they didn't ask to die. They were *made* to. But why, in between, did there have to be such pain? Perhaps humankind was more amusing that way. Perhaps they provided entertainment.

Thorn lay on the couch and slept. And his dreams were filled with fear. He saw himself dressed as a woman, yet knowing he was a man. He was on a crowded street and stopped a policeman, attempting to explain that he was lost and afraid. The policeman refused to listen, instead directing traffic around him until it came so close that he could feel the breeze. The breeze grew in intensity as the traffic moved faster, and Thorn felt as though he were caught in a gale. So strong was the wind that he could not catch his breath, and he gasped, hanging onto the policeman who refused to acknowledge he was there. He cried out for help, but no one could hear him, his cries drowned out by the howling wind. A black car suddenly swerved toward him and he struggled to get out of its way. But the wind pushed him on all sides, holding him in place. As it bore down, he could see the driver's face. It had no features, yet it emitted a laugh, the flesh ripping open where a mouth should have been, spewing blood, as the car came bearing down.

At the moment of contact, Thorn awakened. He was gasping for breath and bathed in sweat. Slowly the dream left him and he lay immobile. It was early morning, and the house was quiet. He fought the urge to weep.

Scenes on the following pages
are from the 20th Century-Fox film, THE OMEN.

Jeremy Thorn, Ambassador to the Court of St. James (Gregory
Peck), his wife Katherine (Lee Remick), and their son Damien
(Harvey Stephens).

Damien and his nanny, Chessa (Holly Palance), at his birthday
party.

The bizarre death of the nanny, as Katherine, with Damien, watches horrified.

Thorn and Katherine try to smooth out the problems in their marriage.

At the zoo, the animals go into a death frenzy at the sight of Damien.

The tragic "accidental" impalement of the mysterious priest, Father Tassone (Patrick Troughton).

Thorn, investigating, visits Tassone's flat, crammed with relics to ward off evil.

What caused Katherine's fall? Another "accident"?

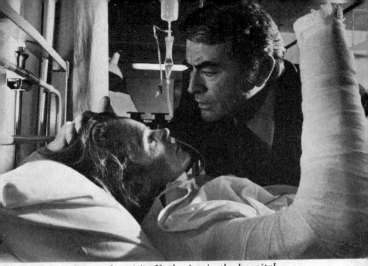

Thorn, distraught, visits Katherine in the hospital.

In an Italian monastery, Thorn questions the burned, blind Father Spilletto (Martin Benson).

Thorn and Jennings, a photographer (David Warner), break open a grave for clues to the mystery of Damien's birth.

In Jerusalem, Jennings is the victim of another incredible "accident."

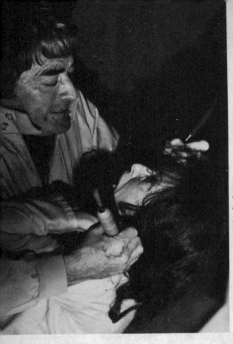

Thorn locked in a death struggle with Damien's sinister second nanny, Mrs. Baylock (Billie Whitelaw).

Would the evil never end?

Chapter Seven

Thorn's speech to the businessmen was at the Mayfair Hotel; by seven o'clock the convention room was filled to capacity. He had told his aides he wanted press coverage, so they had planted an item in the afternoon papers, and now people were being turned away at the door. There were not only the expected attendees, but plenty of reporters as well, even a group of street people who were allowed to stand at the back. The Communist party had taken a keen interest in Thorn, twice sending representatives to heckle and interrupt when he had spoken outdoors, and he hoped they would not be there tonight.

As he strode to the lectern, Thorn noticed, crouched among a small group of photographers, the one whose camera he had broken in front of the Embassy. The photographer smiled at him, holding up a new camera, and Thorn returned the smile, appreciative of the peace-making gesture. Then he waited for the hall to fall silent, and launched into his speech. He spoke of the world economic structure and the importance of the Common Market. In any society, he said, even prehistoric, the marketplace was the common ground, the equalizer of wealth, the melding place of disparate cultures. When one needs to buy, and the other needs to sell, we have the basic components of peace. When one needs to buy and the other *refuses* to sell, we have taken the first step toward war. He spoke of the community of mankind, the need to recognize that we are brethren, sharing an earth whose resources were meant for all.

"We are caught together," he said, quoting Henry

Beston, "in the net of life and time. We are fellow prisoners of the splendor and travail of the earth."

It was an inspiring speech, and the audience hung on every word. The discourse turned toward political turmoil and its relationship to economy, Thorn singling out the faces of the Arabs in the audience and speaking directly to them.

"We can well understand the relationship of turmoil to poverty," he said, "but we must also be mindful that civilizations have been toppled by grievances born of too much *luxury*!"

Thorn was in high gear now, and from a position at his feet, Jennings the photographer focused tight on his face and began snapping photos.

"It is a sad and ironic truth," continued Thorn, "dating as far back as King Solomon's time in Egypt, that those born to wealth and position . . ."

"You should know something about that!" shouted a voice from the back. And Thorn paused, squinting into the darkness of the auditorium. The voice did not come again and Thorn continued.

". . . dating as far back as the Pharaohs' time in Egypt, we find that those born to wealth and position . . ."

"Tell us about it!" called the heckler again, and this time there was an angry stir in the audience; Thorn strained to see. It was a student. He was bearded, in blue jeans, probably from the Communist faction. "What do you know about poverty, Thorn?" he taunted. "You'll never have to work a day in your life!"

The audience hissed their resentment at the heckler, some shouting at him, but Thorn raised his hands for calm.

"The young man has something to say. Let's hear him out."

The youth stepped forward and Thorn waited for him to continue. He would let him rant until he was ranted out.

"If you're so concerned about sharing the wealth, why don't you share some of yours?" shouted the boy. "How many millions do you *have*? Do you know how many people are *starving*? Do you know what the change you're carrying in your pocket could do? With what you pay your chauffeur you could feed a family in India for a month! The grass on your forty-acre-front lawn could feed half the population of Bangladesh! The money you throw away on parties for your child could found a clinic right here in the south end of London! If you're going to urge people to give away their wealth, let's see an example! Don't stand there in your four-hundred-dollar suit and tell us what poverty is about!"

The assault was impassioned. The boy clearly scored. From the audience came a smattering of light applause and it was Thorn's turn to reply.

"Are you through?" asked Thorn.

"What are you worth, Thorn?" shouted the youth. "As much as Rockefeller?"

"Nowhere near."

"When Rockefeller was appointed Vice-President, the papers listed his income as slightly over three hundred million! You know what the slightly *over* was? Thirty-three million! Not even worth counting! That was his *spare change*, while half the population of the world died of starvation! Isn't there something obscene here? Does anyone need as much money as that?"

"I am not Mr. Rockefeller . . ."

"The hell you aren't!"

"Will you let me answer, please?"

"One child! One starving child! Do something for just one starving child! Then we'll believe you! Just reach out with your own hand, not your mouth, with your hand, and extend it to one starving child!"

"Perhaps I've done that," replied Thorn quietly.

"Where is he, then?" demanded the boy. "Who's the

child? Who've you saved, Thorn? Who are you trying to save?"

"Certain of us have responsibilities that extend beyond one starving child."

"You can't save the world, Thorn, until you reach out for that first starving child."

The audience was with the heckler now. He was responded to with a firm and sudden applause.

"You have me at a disadvantage," said Thorn evenly. "You stand in the dark and hurl invective . . ."

"Then turn on the lights, I'll hurl it louder!"

The audience laughed and the houselights began to flicker on, the reporters and photographers suddenly rising, turning their attention to the back of the room. Jennings, the photographer, cursed himself for not having a long lens, and he focused on several heads, the angry youth centered among them.

On the stage, Thorn remained calm, but as the lights came up full, his manner suddenly changed. His eyes were not on the boy, but on another figure, hidden in the shadows some distance behind him. It was the figure of a priest, small in stature, a hat clutched tensely in his hand. It was Tassone. Even though Thorn could not see his features, he knew it was he, and it rendered him immobile.

"What's the matter, Thorn?" taunted the youth. "Nothing to say?"

Thorn's energy was suddenly gone, a wave of fear sweeping over him as he stood mute, gazing into the shadows. From a position beneath him, Jennings swung his camera in the direction of Thorn's fearful gaze, snapping off a series of shots.

"Come on, Thorn!" demanded the heckler. "You can see me now, what do you have to say?"

"I think . . ." said Thorn, faltering, ". . . your points are well taken. We should all share our wealth. I'll try to do more."

The boy was taken off guard, and so was the audience. Someone called for the lights to be switched out, and Thorn returned to his lectern. He struggled to find his place and then gazed up again into the darkness. And in a distant shaft of light, he could see the robes of the one who stalked him.

Jennings had returned late that night and put his films into the developer. The Ambassador had, as usual, impressed and intrigued him. He could spot fear as surely as a rat could smell cheese, and it was fear that he had seen through the viewfinder of his camera. It was not nameless fear, for it was evident that Thorn had seen something, or someone, in the darkness of the auditorium. The light had been poor and the camera angle wide, but Jennings had shot in the direction of the Ambassador's gaze and hoped he would find something when the film was developed. As he waited, he became aware that he was hungry and tore open a sack of groceries he'd bought on his way back from the hotel. He'd purchased a small barbecued chicken and a large bottle of root beer, and he set them out before him for a feast. The chicken was whole save for head and feet, and Jennings stuck it on the end of the root beer bottle so it sat upright, staring headlessly at him across the table. It was a mistake, for he could not eat it now, and instead reached over and flapped its little barbecued wings, and squawked a little as though it were talking. Then he opened a can of sardines and ate in silence with his mute dinner companion.

The timer went off and Jennings moved into the darkroom, using tongs to lift his proofsheets from the acid baths. What he saw brought jubilation, and he howled with joy. Turning on a bright light and slipping the sheet under a magnifying stand, he scrutinized the photos, shaking his head with delight. It was the series of shots taken of the back of the hall. Though not a single face or body could be made out in the darkness,

87

there hung the javelin-like appendage, standing out like a puff of gray smoke.

"Fuck!" muttered Jennings as his eye came upon something else. It was a fat man smoking a cigar. The appendage might indeed be smoke. Racking up his negatives, he singled out the three in question and put them in the enlarger, waiting an agonizing fifteen minutes until they were ready and could be viewed. No. It was not smoke. The color and texture were different, and so was the relative distance to the camera. If it were cigar smoke, the fat man would have had to blow a great quantity of it to create such a cloud. It would have disturbed the people around him, and they were instead completely oblivious of the smoking man, gazing ahead, unperturbed. The ghostlike appendage seemed to be hanging far back in the auditorium, perhaps against the far wall. Jennings slipped the enlargement under his magnifying stand and studied it in great detail. Beneath it he saw the hem of priestly robes. He raised his arms and let out a war cry. It was the little priest again, and he was somehow involved with Thorn.

"Holy *shit*!" cried Jennings. "Hot holy shit!"

And in celebration he returned to the dinner table, ripping off the wings of his silent companion, devouring them to the bones.

"I'm gonna find that sucker!" he laughed. "I'm gonna go hunt him down!"

The following morning he cropped a shot of the priest, one he had taken with the Marine on the Embassy stairs. He took it around to several churches, then finally to the regional offices of the London Parish. But no one recognized the photo, assuring Jennings that if the priest were employed in the area, they would have known him. He was from outside the city somewhere. The job would be harder. On a hunch, Jennings went to Scotland Yard and got access to their mug books, but it turned up nothing, and he knew there was only one thing left to do. He had first seen the priest coming out of the Embassy; probably someone in there would know.

It was difficult to gain entrance to the Embassy. Security guards checked credentials and appointments, and they wouldn't let Jennings past the front desk.

"I'd like to see the Ambassador," Jennings explained. "He said he'd reimburse me for a camera."

They called upstairs, and to Jennings' surprise they told him to go to a lobby phone where the Ambassador's office would call him. Jennings did as he was instructed, and in a moment was speaking to Thorn's secretary who wanted to know the sum involved and where a check should be mailed.

"I'd like to explain it to him personally," said Jennings. "I'd like to show him what he's getting for his money."

She replied that that would be impossible as the Ambassador was in a meeting, and Jennings decided to go for broke.

"To tell you the truth, I thought he could help me with a personal problem. Maybe you could help me instead. I'm looking for a priest. He's a relative. He's had some business at the Embassy, and I thought maybe someone here had seen him and could help me."

It was an odd request and the secretary was reluctant to respond.

"He's a very short fella," added Jennings.

"Is he Italian?" she asked.

"I think he spent some time in Italy," replied Jennings, faking it to see what it was worth.

"Would his name be Tassone?" asked the secretary.

"Well, actually, I'm not sure. See, what I'm doing is trying to trace a lost relative. My mother's brother was separated from her as a child and changed his last name. My mother is dying now and she wants to find him. We don't know his last name, we only have a vague description. We know he's small like my mother, and we know he became a priest, and a friend of mine saw a priest leaving the Embassy a week or so ago, and this friend said the priest looked exactly like my mother."

"There was a priest here," said the secretary. "He said he was from Rome, and I believe his name was Tassone."

"Do you know where he lives?"

"No."

"He had business with the Ambassador?"

". . . I believe so."

"Maybe the Ambassador knows where he lives."

"I wouldn't know. I don't think so."

"Would it be possible to ask him?"

"I guess I could."

"When could you do that?"

"Well, not until later."

"My mother's very sick. She's in the hospital now and I'm afraid the time is growing short."

In Thorn's office, the intercom buzzed; a secretary's voice inquired whether he knew how to contact the priest who had been to see him two weeks before. Thorn paused in his work, suddenly going cold.

"Who's asking?"

"A man who says you broke his camera. The priest is a relative of his. Or he thinks he is."

After a momentary pause, Thorn replied. "Would you ask him to come up, please."

Jennings found his way to Thorn's office with no trouble. Modernistic, it was plainly the office of the man in charge. It was at the end of a long hall adorned with portraits of all the American ambassadors to London. As Jennings moved by them, he was interested to find that John Quincy Adams and James Monroe had held the post before becoming President. Maybe it was a good stepping-stone at that. Perhaps old Thorn *was* destined for greatness.

"Come in," smiled Thorn. "Have a seat."

"Sorry to bust in . . ."

"Not at all."

The Ambassador gestured Jennings forward, and he entered, finding a chair. In all of his years of stalking, this was the first time he'd ever made personal contact with his prey. It was easy to talk his way in, but now he was shaken, his heart racing, his knees unsteady. He'd remembered feeling this way the first time he developed a photo. The excitement was so great it was almost sexual in nature.

"I've been wanting to apologize about that camera," said Thorn.

"It was an old one anyway."

"I want to reimburse you."

"No, no . . ."

"I'd like to. I'd like to make it up to you."

Jennings shrugged and nodded his okay.

"Why don't you just tell me what the best kind of camera is, and I'll have someone get it for you."

"Well, that's very generous . . ."

"Just tell me the best there is."

"It's a German make. Pentaflex. Three Hundred."

"Done. Just let my secretary know where we can find you."

Jennings nodded again, and the men eyed each other in silence. Thorn was studying him, sizing him up, taking in everything from the unmatched socks to the threads hanging off the collar of his jacket. Jennings liked this kind of scrutiny. He knew his appearance put people off. In a perverse way, it gave him an edge.

"I've seen you around," said Thorn.

"That's where I try to be."

"You're very dilligent."

"Thank you."

Thorn stepped from behind his desk, moving to a cabinet where he uncorked a bottle of brandy. Jennings watched him pour, accepting a glass.

"Thought you handled that boy very well the other night," said Jennings.

"Did you?"

"I did."

"I'm not sure."

They were killing time, both sensing it, each waiting for the other to get to the point.

"I *sided* with him," added Thorn. "Pretty soon the press will be calling me a Communist."

"Oh, you know the press."

"Yes."

"Got to make a living."

"Right."

They sipped their brandy, and Thorn moved to the windows, gazing out.

"You're looking for a relative?"

"Yes, sir."

"He's a priest named Tassone?"

"He's a priest, but I'm not sure of his name. My mother's brother. Separated when they were children."

Thorn glanced at Jennings, and Jennings sensed his disappointment.

"So you don't actually know him," said the Ambassador.

"No, sir. I'm trying to find him."

Thorn frowned and sat heavily in his chair.

"If I might inquire . . ." asked Jennings. "Maybe if I knew what his business was with you . . ."

"It was business about a hospital. He wanted . . . a donation."

"What hospital?"

"Oh, in Rome. I'm not sure."

"Did he leave you his address?"

"No. As a matter of fact I'm a little upset about that. I promised I'd send a check and I don't know where to send it."

Jennings nodded. "Guess we're in the same boat, then."

"I guess we are," responded Thorn.

"He just came and went, is that it?"

"Yes."

"And you never saw him again?"

Thorn's jaw tightened, and Jennings caught it, seeing clearly that the Ambassador was hiding something.

"Never again."

"Thought maybe . . . he might have attended one of your speeches."

Their eyes caught and held, Thorn sensing he was being played with.

"What's your name?" asked Thorn.

"Jennings. Haber Jennings."

"Mr. Jennings . . ."

"Haber."

"Haber."

Thorn studied the man's face, then averted his eyes, again looking out the window.

"Sir?"

". . . I have a great interest in finding this man. The priest who was here. I'm afraid I was abrupt with him and I'd like to make amends."

"Abrupt in what way?"

"I dismissed him rather rudely. I didn't really hear what he had to say."

"I'm sure he's used to it. When you hit people up for donations . . ."

"I'd like to find him. It's important to me."

From the look on Thorn's face, it plainly was. Jennings knew he'd stumbled into something, but he didn't know what. All he could do was play it straight.

"If I locate him, I'll let you know," he said.

"Would you please?"

"Of course."

Thorn nodded with finality, and Jennings rose, and walking over to Thorn, shook his hand.

"You look very worried, Mr. Ambassador. I hope the world's not about to explode."

"Oh, no," responded Thorn with a smile.

"I'm an admirer of yours. That's why I follow you around."

"Thank you."

Jennings headed for the door, but Thorn stopped him.

"Mr. Jennings?"

"Sir?"

"Let me understand . . . you've never actually seen this priest yourself?"

"No."

"You made that remark about his being at one of my speeches. I thought perhaps . . ."

"No."

"Well. No matter."

There was an uncomfortable pause, then Jennings again moved to the door.

"Any chance I could take some pictures of you? I mean at home? With your family?"

"It's not a good time right now."

"Maybe I'll call in a few weeks."

"Do that."

"You'll hear from me."

He left and Thorn gazed after him. The man clearly knew something that he wasn't divulging. But what could he possibly know about the priest? Was it mere coincidence that a man he'd had random contact with was seeking the priest who followed and haunted him? Thorn tried hard but could make no sense of it. Like so many other recent events in his life, it seemed like mere coincidence but was somehow something more.

Chapter Eight

For Edgardo Emilio Tassone, life on earth could have been no worse than that in purgatory. It was for that reason that he, as so many others, had joined the coven in Rome. He was Portuguese by birth, the son of a fisherman who died off the Grand Banks of New-foundland while fishing for cod. His memory of child-hood was the smell of fish. It clung to his mother like a cloak of sickness, and in fact she had died of a parasite ingested from eating fish raw when she became too weak to forage for firewood. Orphaned at the age of eight, Tassone was taken to a monastery; there, beaten by monks until he confessed his sins, he was saved. He had embraced Christ by the time he was ten, but by then his back was scarred from the penance it took to make the Holy One finally appear.

With the fear of God literally beaten into him, he devoted his life to the Church, remaining eight years in the seminary, studying the Bible day and night. He read of God's love and God's anger, and at the age of twenty-five ventured forth into the world to save others from the fires of Hell. He became a missionary, going first to Spain, then to Morocco, preaching the word of the Lord. From Morocco he traveled into the southeast corner of Africa, there finding heathens to convert, and he converted them in the way he himself was. He beat them as he was beaten and came to realize that in the heat of religious ecstasy he took sexual pleasure in their pain. Among the young African converts, one came to worship him, and they shared carnal pleasure, defiling the primitive laws of Man and God. The boy's name was Tobu, of the Kikuyu tribe. When he and Tassone

were found together, the boy was ceremonially muti-
lated, his scrotum opened and his testicles removed;
the boy was forced to eat them while his warrior brothers looked on. Tassone himself barely escaped, word
reaching him in Somalia that the Kikuyu had seized a
Franciscan monk and skinned him alive in Tassone's
stead. After skinning him, they made him walk until he
finally fell dead.

Tassone fled to Djibouti, then Adan, then Djakarta,
feeling God's wrath upon him wherever he went. Death
stalked him, striking those around him, and he feared
that at any moment he would be next. He knew well,
from his biblical texts, of the wrath of a God scorned,
and he moved fast, seeking protection from what he
knew must inevitably come. In Nairobi he met the
graceful Father Spilletto and confessed his sins;
Spilletto promised to protect him and took him to
Rome. It was there, in the coven in Rome, that he
was indoctrinated into the dogma of Hell. The Satanists provided a sanctuary where the judgment of God
did not exist. They lived for the pursuit of bodily
pleasure, and Tassone shared his body with others
whose pleasure matched his. They were a community
of outcasts who, together, could cast out the rest. The
Devil was worshipped by the desecration of God.

The coven was made up mostly of working class
people, but a few were professional, highly placed men.
On the outside they all led respectable lives; this was
their most valuable weapon against those who worshipped God. It was their mission to create fear and
turmoil, to turn men against each other until the time
of the Unholy One had come; small groups called Task
Forces would forage out to create chaos wherever
possible. The coven in Rome took credit for much of
the turmoil in Ireland, using random sabotage to polar-
ize Catholics and Prostestants and fan the fires of religious war. Two Irish nuns, known within the coven as
B'aalock and B'aalam, had orchestrated the bombings

in Ireland, the one known as B'aalam having died by her own hand. Her body was found in the rubble of a marketplace explosion, the remains returned to Italy where they were buried in the hallowed ground of Cerveteri, the ancient Etruscan graveyard, known today as Cimitero di Sant'Angelo, on the outskirts of Rome.

For her devotion to the Unholy One, B'aalam was honored by being entombed beneath the Shrine of Techulca, the Etruscan Devil-God, and members of surrounding covens attended the funeral, numbering almost five thousand strong. Tassone was impressed by the ceremony, and thereafter became politically active in the coven, seeking to aggrandize himself and prove to Spilletto he was worthy of trust.

The first demonstration of this trust came in 1968 when, with another priest, Tassone was dispatched by Spilletto to Southeast Asia; there, organizing a small band of mercenaries in Communist-held Cambodia, he crossed into and disrupted the cease-fire in South Vietnam. The North blamed it on the South, the South on the North, and within days of Tassone's entrance, the hard-won peace was shattered. The coven believed it would pave the way for an all-out Communist takeover in Southeast Asia; Cambodia, Laos, Vietnam, then Thailand and the Philippines as well. It was hoped that in a few short years the mere mention of the word "God" would be considered heresy throughout the entire southeastern hemisphere.

Within the coven there was much celebration, and Tassone returned to find himself a leader of his cult. The fires of unrest were brewing in Africa and, aware of his knowledge of that country, Spilletto sent Tassone to assist the revolution that eventually brought Idi Amin, the insane African despot, to power. Though Tassone, being white, was not trusted by Amin, he remained there for over a year, successfully lobbying for Amin's political takeover of the Caucus of African Nations.

Largely because of Tassone's accomplishments, the coven in Rome became looked upon by Satanists across the world as the seat of political direction and spiritual power, and money began to flow there, adding to their strength. Rome itself was a hotbed of energy: the seat of Catholicism, the seat of western Communism, the core of Satanism throughout the world. The atmosphere fairly crackled with power.

It was at this time, at the height of Satanic strength and world turmoil, that the biblical symbols fell into place heralding the moment when earth history would suddenly and irrevocably change. For the third time since the formation of the planet, the Evil One would spew forth his progeny, entrusting its nurturing to maturity to his disciples on earth. It had been attempted twice before without success; the watchdogs of Christ discovered the Beast and killed it before it came into power. This time it would not fail. The concept was right; the plan timed to perfection.

It was no surprise that Spilletto chose Tassone as one of the three to carry out the momentous plan. The small, scholarly priest was loyal, dedicated, and followed orders without the slightest hesitation or remorse. For this reason his part would be the most brutal; the murder of the innocent who, by necessity, had to be involved. It was Spilletto who would choose the surrogate family and he who would effect the transfer of the child. Sister Maria Teresa (which was now what the woman B'aalock was called) would tend the impregnation and assist in the birth. Tassone would supervise the grisly aftermath, making sure the evidence would disappear and be buried in hallowed ground.

Tassone entered into the covenant eagerly, for he saw clearly that his life was now given to the ages. He would be remembered and revered; he, once a cast-off orphan, now one of the Chosen Ones, was allowed to enter into an alliance with the devil himself. But in the days preceding the event, something began to happen to Tassone; his strength began to falter. The scars on his back started to pain him, the agony becoming more intense with each passing night as he lay awake in his bed desperately searching for sleep. For five nights he tossed fitfully, fighting disturbing illusions that flew through his mind, and he sought herbal potions that brought slumber, but did nothing to quiet the nightmares that visited him as he slept.

He saw visions of Tobu, the African boy, pleading with him, begging him for help. And he saw the skinless form of a man, eye sockets gaping above peeled ligament and muscle, a mouth without lips crying out for mercy. Tassone saw himself as a boy, waiting on the beach for the return of his father, and then he saw his mother on her deathbed, begging for forgiveness for dying, for deserting him so young and abandoning him to fate. He awoke that night crying out, as though he were his own mother, pleading to be forgiven. And when he lapsed again into slumber, the figure of Christ appeared beside him, assuring him that he would be forgiven. Christ in all his boyish beauty, his slim body still bearing scars, knelt by Tassone and told him he was still welcome in the Kingdom of Heaven. All he had to do was repent.

The nightmares had shaken Tassone, and Spilletto sensed the tension, summoning him to his quarters to find the reason for it. But Tassone was in too deeply now, knowing his life would be in danger if he betrayed any doubt, and he assured Spilletto he was eager still to do what had to be done. It was the pain in his back that was bothering him, he said, and Spilletto offered him a vial of pills to bring relief. From then on, until the act was at hand, Tassone rested in a state of drugged tranquility, and the disquieting visions of Christ ceased to haunt him.

The night of June sixth. The sixth month, the sixth day, the sixth hour. Events occurred that would follow Tassone to the end of his days. In the midst of labor the surrogate mother had begun to wail, Sister Maria Teresa silencing it with ether as its giant progeny tore through the womb. Tassone finished the job for her with the stone given to him by Spilletto. He crushed the animal's head to a pulp, and it prepared him for what had to be done to the human child. But when the newborn human child was brought down to him, he hesitated, for it was a child of uncommon beauty. He gazed at them both, the two infants side by side: the blood-covered one, thick with hair; and the soft, white, beautiful one, its eyes gazing upward in absolute trust. He knew what had to be done, and he did it, but he did not do it well. It had to be redone, and he sobbed as he tore open the crate to hit the Thorn child once again. For an instant he was gripped by the impulse to grab the child up in his arms, to run with it and keep running, to find a place of safety. But he saw the infant was already damaged, irreparably so, and the stone came down hard again. And again. And again. Until the sound had stopped and the body lay still.

In the darkness of that night, no one saw the tears that streamed down Tassone's face; in fact, from that night on, no one in the coven ever saw him again. He fled Rome the following morning and lived in obscurity for the four years that passed. Going to Belgium, he worked among the poor, finding his way to a clinic where he could get access to the drugs he needed not only to quiet the pain in his back but to fight the haunting memories of what he had done. He lived alone and spoke to no one, gradually becoming infirm. And when he finally entered a hospital, a diagnosis was quickly confirmed. The pain in his back was caused by a tumor; malignant and inoperable because of its position on the spine.

Tassone was dying now, and it was this that drove him to seek forgiveness from the Lord. Christ was good. Christ would forgive. He would prove himself worthy of that forgiveness by attempting to undo what he had done.

Summoning what little strength remained, he traveled to Israel, carrying with him eight vials of morphine to deaden the pain that throbbed in his back. He was seeking the man named Bugenhagen, a name linked with Satan almost since the beginning of time. It was a Bugenhagen who, in the year 1092, found the first progeny of Satan and devised the means of putting it to death. It was again a Bugenhagen in 1710 who found the second issue and damaged it to the point where it could summon no earthly power. They were religious zealots, the watchdogs of Christ; their mission, to keep the Unholy One from walking the face of the earth.

It took Tassone seven months to find the last descendant of the Bugenhagens, for he lived in obscurity, ensconced in a fortress beneath the surface of the earth. Here he, like Tassone, waited for death, tortured with the infirmities of age and the knowledge that he had failed. He, like so many others, had known the time was at hand but he was helpless to stop the son of Satan from being born unto the earth.

Tassone spent but six hours with the old man, recounting the story and his part in the birth. Bugenhagen listened with despair as the priest begged him to intervene. For he could not. He was imprisoned here in his fortress and dared not venture to the outside. Someone with direct access to the child would have to be brought to him.

Fearing his time was short. Tassone made his way to London to find Thorn and convince him of what must be done. He prayed that God was watching him and he feared that Satan was watching him as well. But he was not ignorant of the Devil's work and took every precaution to maintain life and breath until he could find Thorn and his story could be told. If he could do this, he knew he would be absolved of his sins and admitted into the Kingdom of Heaven.

Renting a one-room flat in Soho, he made it into a fortress as secure as a church. His armament was the scriptures; he covered every inch of wall space, even the windows, with pages torn from the Bible. It took seventy Bibles to do it all. Crosses hung everywhere, at all angles, and he made sure never to venture out unless his crucifix, impregnated with particles of broken mirror, could reflect the sunlight as it hung about his neck.

But he found that his quarry was hard to reach, and the pain in his back was all-consuming. The one meeting with Thorn, in his office, was a failure. He had frightened the Ambassador and was summarily dismissed. Now he followed him everywhere, his desperation growing; and this day he stood watching the Ambassador from the opposite side of a chain-link fence, as Thorn and a group of dignitaries dedicated a housing project in a poor section of Chelsea.

"I'm proud to dedicate this particular project . . ." shouted Thorn against the wind to the hundred or so people looking on, ". . . as it represents the will of the community itself to improve the quality of life!"

So saying, he dug a shovel into the earth; an accordion band struck up a polka as he and the group of dignitaries were led toward the chain-link fence to shake hands with people who reached through, straining to touch them as they neared. He was a consummate politician, a man who enjoyed adulation, and as he moved by the fence he made an effort to shake each of the greedy hands, even bending close to be kissed by a pair of eager protruding lips. But suddenly he was jarred; a hand reached through with sudden violence and grabbing him hard by the shirt-front, pulled him close to the fence.

"Tomorrow," panted Tassone into the Ambassador's frightened eyes. "One o'clock, Kew Gardens. . . ."

"Unhand me!" gasped Thorn.

"Five minutes, then you'll never see me again."

"Get your hands . . ."

"Your wife is in danger. She'll die unless you come."

As Thorn pulled back, the priest was suddenly gone; the Ambassador was left dazed, gazing into strange faces, flashbulbs going off in his eyes.

Thorn had struggled as to what to do about the priest. He could simply send the police in his stead, and they could take Tassone to jail. But the charge would be harassment, and Thorn, as complainant, would have to appear. The priest would be interrogated. The issue would become public. The newspapers would have a feast, capitalizing on the rantings of an insane man. He couldn't have it. Not now, not ever. There was no way of knowing what the priest would say. His fixation centered around the birth of the child; a macabre coincidence that it was an area in which Thorn had something to hide. As an alternative to the police, perhaps Thorn could send an emissary to pay the man off, or threaten him into going away. But that would also mean involving an outsider.

He thought of Jennings, the photographer, and almost followed the impulse to call him, to tell him he had located the man he was looking for. But that wouldn't do either. There could be nothing more dangerous than involving a member of the press. Yet he wished there were *someone*. Someone he could share it with. For in truth he was frightened. He was afraid of what the priest would say.

Thorn took his own car that morning, explaining to Horton that he wanted some time to be by himself, and he drove all morning, avoiding the office, for fear he would be questioned about where he was going for lunch. It occurred to him that he could simply *ignore* the priest's demand, that the rebuff might finally make him lose interest and go away. But that wasn't satisfactory either, for Thorn *himself* sought the confrontation. He needed to face the man down and hear everything he had to say. He had said Katherine was in danger, that she would die unless Thorn came. It was not possible that Katherine was in danger, but it pained Thorn that she too had become a focal point in the demented man's mind.

Thorn arrived at twelve thirty, parked by the curb, and waited tensely in his car. The time passed slowly, and he listened to the news, only half-hearing as the roll call of countries in trouble was sounded. Spain, Lebanon, Laos, Belfast, Angola, Zaire, Israel, Thailand. One could literally close his eyes and point to the map and be within inches, at most, of a hot spot. It seemed the longer man's time on earth, the shorter the outlook for habitation. The time-bomb was ticking and one of these days it would go off. Plutonium, the by-product of nuclear power, was now available to everyone, and with it, even the smallest countries could arm themselves for atomic war. Some were bent, anyway, on suicidal destruction. They would lose nothing if in their outrage they took the rest of the world with them. Thorn thought of the Sinai Desert, the Promised Land. He wondered if God knew when he promised it to Abraham that it was there that the time-bomb would go off.

He gazed at the clock on his dashboard; it was one o'clock. Pulling himself together, he slowly entered the park. He had worn a raincoat and dark glasses so as not to be recognized, but the disguise added to his anxiety as he searched for the figure of the priest. He spotted him, and froze, fighting off the impulse to go no farther. Tassone was alone on a bench, his back to him; Thorn could easily have turned without being seen. But instead he moved forward, circling the priest and confronting him head on.

Tassone was jarred by Thorn's sudden appearance; his face was tense and bathed in sweat, as though suffering unendurable pain. For a long moment, they stared in silence.

"I should have brought the police," said Thorn curtly.

"They can't help you."

"Get on with it. Say what you have to say."

Tassone's eyes fluttered and his hands began to tremble. He was plainly under intense exertion; the exertion of fighting pain.

"When the Jews return to Zion . . ." he whispered.

"What?"

". . . When the Jews return to Zion. And a comet fills the sky. And the Holy Roman Empire rises. Then you and I . . . must die."

Thorn's heart leapt. The man *was* insane. It was a *poem* he was reciting, his face rigid and trancelike, his voice rising in shrill intensity.

"From the Eternal Sea he rises. Creating armies on either shore. Turning man against his brother. Till man exists no more!"

Thorn watched as the priest began to quake in every fiber, struggling to make himself heard.

"The Book of Revelations predicted it all!" he blurted.

"I'm not here for a religious sermon."

"It is by means of a human personality entirely in his possession that Satan will wage his last and most formidable offense. Book of Daniel, Book of Luke . . ."

"You said my wife was in danger."

"Go to the town of Meggido," entreated Tassone. "In the old city of Jezreel. There see the old man Bugenhagen. He alone can describe how the child must die."

"Look here . . ."

"He who will not be saved by the Lamb will be torn by the Beast!"

"Stop it!"

Tassone fell silent, his posture sagging as he raised a

trembling hand to wipe perspiration that had accumulated on his brow.

"I'm here," said Thorn quietly, "because you said my wife was in danger."

"I had a vision, Mr. Thorn."

"You said my wife . . ."

"She is pregnant!"

Thorn was stopped, taken aback.

"You're mistaken."

"I believe she is pregnant."

"She's not."

"He will not allow the child to be born. He will kill it while it slumbers in the womb."

The priest groaned, struck again by violent pain.

"What are you talking about?" asked Thorn under his breath.

"Your *son*, Mr. Thorn! The son of *Satan*! He will kill the unborn child and then he will kill your wife! And when he is certain to inherit all that is yours, then, Mr. Thorn, he will kill *you*!"

"That's enough!"

". . . And with your wealth and power he will establish his counterfeit Kingdom here on earth, receiving his orders directly from Satan."

"You're *insane*," hissed Thorn.

"He must *die*, Mr. Thorn!"

The priest gasped and a tear slipped from his eye; Thorn gazed down at him, unable to move.

"Please, Mr. Thorn . . ." the priest wept.

"You asked for five minutes . . ."

"Go to the city of Meggido," Tassone begged. "See Bugenhagen before it's too late!"

Thorn shook his head, pointing a trembling finger at the priest.

"I've heard you, now . . ." he warned. "I want you to hear *me*. If I ever see you again . . . I'll have you arrested."

Turning on his heel, he began to move away, Tassone calling after him through his tears.

"You'll see me in Hell, Mr. Thorn. There we will share our sentence!"

In a moment, Thorn was gone; Tassone was left alone, his head in his hands. He remained there for several minutes, trying to stop the tears. But they would not stop. It was over and he had failed.

Rising slowly, he gazed about the park. It was empty now and quiet; the stillness was somehow ominous. It was as though he stood in a vacuum, the very air holding its breath. Then, faintly, he began to hear the sound. It was distant at first, almost subliminal, gradually growing in intensity until it filled the atmosphere around him. It was the sound of the OHM, and as it continued to rise, Tassone gripped his crucifix, his breath coming short as he gazed fearfully about the park. The sky was darkening and a breeze began to rise, quickly gaining momentum until the tree limbs shook with anger.

Clutching his cross with both hands, Tassone began to move, seeking the safety of the street. But there the wind suddenly rose around him, paper and debris swirling at his feet as he squinted and gasped, a forceful blast rushing at his face. Across the street he could see a church, but as he stepped off the curb the wind suddenly rushed at him with gale force, and he leaned into it, pushing hard against it to make his way to safety. The sound of the OHM was ringing in his ears now, mixed with the sound of howling wind; Tassone moaning with exertion as he struggled forward, his vision obscured by the cloud of swirling dust. He neither saw nor heard the truck barreling down, only the squeal of its massive tires as it swerved within inches, careening into a row of parked cars, then smashing to a sudden stop.

The wind suddenly halted, and people were screaming, running by Tassone toward the crashed truck, where the driver's head hung limply, dripping blood, against the window. A rumble of thunder rolled across the sky as Tassone stood mid-street, whimpering with fear. A bolt of lightning flashed above the distant church, and Tassone wheeled, running back into the park. With a sudden crash of thunder, rain began to pour down, Tassone running in desperation as lightning began striking around him, a large tree fairly exploding as he passed. Crying out with fear, he slipped in mud, struggling to regain his footing as a finger of electricity streaked downward, splintering a park bench to burning matchsticks beside him. Whirling, he crashed through a stand of bushes, emerging on a small sidestreet, and the lightning came again, hitting a mailbox next to him and hurling it into the air, leaving it peeled back like a used sardine can as it rolled and clattered to the ground.

Sobbing, the small priest staggered foreward, his eyes gazing upward into the angry sky. The rain came hard, stinging his face, the city blurred before him in the translucent veil of water. All over London people were scurrying for cover; windows were slamming shut; six blocks away a teacher was struggling with an old-fashioned window pole as, in the din of downpouring rain, her small students looked on. She had never heard of the priest Tassone, nor knew that her fate would be linked with his. But at that moment on the slick and hissing streets, Tassone was making his way inexorably toward her. Gasping for breath, he stumbled down narrow alleyways, running aimlessly, fleeing the wrath that pursued him. The lightning was distant now, but Tassone's strength was failing, his heart stinging within him as he rounded a corner and paused there at the base of a building, his mouth agape, sucking desperately for air. His eyes were fixed on the distant park where lightning still struck with each crash of thunder; he did not think to look up, where a sudden movement occurred above. From a third-story window directly overhead a window pole slipped out, a woman's hands grappling for it as it escaped and plummeted downward, its metal tip cutting air with the directness of an earth-bound javelin. It smashed directly into the priest's head, running the length of his body, impaling him in the grass.

There he hung suspended, his arms akimbo, like a marionette hung up for the night.

All around London, the summer rain suddenly ceased.

From the third floor of a schoolhouse, a teacher stuck her head out the window and began to scream; and on a street on the other side of the park a group of people carried the dead body of a driver from his overturned truck; his forehead bearing the bloodied imprint of the steering wheel against which it had smashed.

As the clouds parted and the sun's rays once again shone peacefully down, a group of small children gathered in silent curiosity around the figure of a priest hung stiffly on a pole. Droplets of rain dripped from his hat, passing a face frozen in an expression of open mouth puzzlement. A horse-fly buzzed about him and lighted on his parted lips.

At the front gate of Pereford the following morning, Horton collected the newspaper and brought it into the sun room where Thorn and Katherine were having breakfast. As he left, Horton noticed that Mrs. Thorn's face was still drawn and etched with tension. She had looked this way for weeks now, and he suspected it had something to do with her regular forays into London to spend time with her doctor. He had at first assumed that the appointments he brought her to were for a physical ailment, but then he saw on the directory in the building's lobby that her Dr. Greer was a psychiatrist. Horton himself had never felt the need for a psychiatrist, nor did he know anyone who did, and he harbored a feeling that they only served to drive people crazy. When one read in the newspapers of people committing atrocities it was often accompanied by the information that they had been seeing a psychiatrist; the cause and effect was clearly plain. Now, as he observed Mrs. Thorn, his theory on psychiatry was being borne out. No matter how cheerful she appeared on the drive into town, she was silent and withdrawn on the way back home.

Since the visits began, her mood had continually darkened, and now she was clearly under a strain. Her relationship with the household staff were limited to terse commands, and her relationship with her child had been all but severed. The unhappy part was that the child himself had begun to want her. The period of weeks she had spent trying to regain his affections had had an effect; but now, as Damien looked about for her, she was nowhere to be found.

For Katherine herself, the therapy had indeed been troubling, for she had scratched the surface of her fears, and found beneath it a bottomless pit of anxiety and despair. The life she led was fraught with confusion, and she felt she no longer knew who she was. She remembered who she *used* to be and what she once wanted, but that was all gone now, and she could envision no future. The simplest things filled her with fear: the phone ringing, the oven timer going off, the teapot whistling as though demanding to be attended to. She was coming to the point where she simply could not cope, and the act of getting through each day required continual courage.

This day took more courage than most, for she had discovered something that demanded action. It required the kind of confrontation with her husband that she feared, and adding to her anxiety was the child. He had made it a habit of hanging close to her in the morning, trying to attract her attention: today he was noisily riding a wheeled car around the parquet floor in the sun room, bumping insistently into her chair and screaming like a train engine as he played.

"Mrs. Baylock?!!" Katherine called.

Thorn, seated across from her unfolding the newspaper, was jolted by the anger of her tone.

"Something wrong?" he asked.

"Damien. I can't stand that noise."

"It's not all that bad . . ."

"Mrs. Baylock!" she called.

The heavyset woman entered at a near run.

"Ma'am?"

"Take him out of here," Katherine commanded.

"He's only playing," objected Thorn.

"I said take him out!"

"Yes, ma'am," replied Mrs. Baylock.

She took Damien by the hand, leading him from the room. As he went, the child gazed back at his mother, his eyes filled with hurt. Thorn saw it, and turned to Katherine with despair. She continued eating, avoiding his eyes.

"Why ever did we have a child, Katherine?"

"Our image," she replied.

". . . What?"

"How could we not have a child, Jeremy? Who ever heard of a beautiful family not having a beautiful child?"

Thorn absorbed it in silence, upset by her tone.

"Katherine . . ."

"It's true, isn't it? We never thought of what it would be like to raise one. We just thought of what our pictures would look like in the newspapers."

Thorn gazed at her dumbfounded; she returned his gaze evenly.

"It's true, isn't it?" she asked.

"Is this what your doctor is doing for you?"

"Yes."

"Then I think I'd better have a word with him."

"Yes, he has something to talk to you about, too."

Her manner was direct and cold. And Thorn instinctively feared what she had to say.

"What would that be?" he asked.

"We have a problem, Jeremy," she said.

". . . Yes?"

"I want no more children. Ever."

Thorn searched her face, waiting for more.

"Is that all right?" she asked.

"If that's what you want," he replied.

"Then you'll agree to an abortion."

Thorn froze. Open-mouthed. Stunned.

"I'm pregnant, Jeremy. I found out yesterday morning."

A silence passed. Thorn's head was reeling.

"Did you hear me?" Katherine asked.

"How can that be?" Thorn whispered.

"It's the coil. It's sometimes not effective."

"You're pregnant?" he gasped.

"Not far."

Thorn was ashen, and his hands trembled as he stared at the table.

"Did you tell anyone?" he asked.

"Just Dr. Greer."

"Are you sure?"

"That I don't want to keep it?"

"That you're pregnant."

"Yes."

Thorn remained immobile, his gaze frozen into space. Beside him the phone rang and, mechanically, he picked it up.

"Yes?" He paused, not recognizing the voice. "Yes, this is he." His eyes became puzzled and he glanced up at Katherine. "What? Who is this? Hello? Hello?"

The caller hung up; Thorn sat unmoving, his eyes filled with alarm.

"What was it?" asked Katherine.

"Something about the newspapers . . ."

"What about the newspapers?"

"Some person just called me . . . and said . . . to 'read' them today."

He looked down at the folded newspaper in front of him and slowly opened it, cringing as his eyes fell on a photo on the front page.

"What is it?" Katherine asked. "What's wrong?"

But he was unable to reply, and she took it from him, finding the object of his gaze. It was a photo of a priest impaled on a window pole, the banner beneath it reading: PRIEST KILLED IN BIZARRE TRAGEDY.

Katherine looked at her husband and saw that he was shaking; in confusion, she reached for his hand. It was cold.

"Jerry . . ."

Thorn rose stiffly and began to move out of the room.

"Did you know him?" asked Katherine.

But he never replied. Katherine looked again at the photo, and as she read the article she heard Thorn's car start, then disappear down the drive.

> For Mrs. James Akrewian, teacher of the third grade, Bishops Industrial School, the day had begun like any other. It was Friday, and when the rain started she was preparing her class for reading aloud. Though no rain was coming in the window, she attempted to close it to shut out the noise. She had complained many times about the antiquated windows, for she could not herself reach the uppermost ones, needing a stool to reach them, even with the pole. Unable to make contact between the metal ring on the window and the hook on the pole, she thrust the pole outward, attempting to catch the back end of the window and pull it toward her. The balance of the pole was upset and it slipped from her grip, falling outward where it hit the passerby who was probably seeking shelter from the rain. The identity of the deceased is being withheld by police pending notification of relatives.

Katherine could make no sense of it and she called Thorn's office, leaving word for him to phone her as soon as he arrived. Apparently he never arrived, for by noon the return call had still not come. She next phoned Greer, her psychiatrist, but he was too busy and could not come to the phone. Her last call was to the hospital to make arrangements for an abortion.

Chapter Nine

After seeing the priest's photo, Thorn had driven fast toward London, his mind racing in an attempt to sort things out. Katherine *was* pregnant, the priest had been right. And now he could no longer dismiss the rest of what Tassone had said. He tried to recall their meeting in the park: the names, the places that Tassone said he should go. He fought for calm, trying to register each recent event: the conversation with Katherine, the anonymous phone call. "Read the papers," the voice had said. The voice was familiar, but Thorn could not nail it down. Who on the face of this earth knew he was involved with the priest? The photographer. That was the voice. It was Haber Jennings.

Going to his office, Thorn closeted himself alone. Buzzing his secretary on the intercom, he asked her to get Jennings on the phone. She tried but received a tape-recorded message that Jennings was out. She reported this to Thorn, mentioning the tape recording; Thorn requested the number and dialed it himself. The recording was in Jennings' own voice, one of the do-it-yourself answering services. It was the same voice that called him. Why had he not identified himself? What kind of game was he playing?

Thorn next received word that Katherine had called, but he delayed calling her back. She would want to talk about the abortion and he was not ready to reply.

"He will kill it," Thorn remembered the priest saying. "He will kill it while it slumbers in the womb."

Thorn quickly found the phone number of Dr. Charles Greer and explained he was on his way over on a matter of urgency.

Thorn's visit came as no surprise to Greer, for the doctor had sensed Katherine's deterioration. There was a fine line between anxiety and desperation, and he had seen her, several times, jump back and forth across the line. Her terror could become extreme, and it occurred to him that she might try to take her life.

"One never knows how deep these fears go," he said to Thorn in his office. "But frankly I'd be remiss if I didn't confess I think she's headed for serious emotional trouble."

Thorn sat tensely in a hard-backed chair, while the young psychiatrist puffed hard on his pipe trying to keep it lit as he moved about the room.

"I've seen it before," he continued. "It's like a freight train. You can just watch it picking up steam."

"She's gotten worse then?" Thorn asked in a shaky voice.

"Let's say it's developing."

"There's nothing you can do?"

"I see her twice a week. I think she needs more constant care."

"Are you telling me she's insane?"

"Let's say she's living in her fantasies. Her fantasies are terrifying. She's responding to that terror."

"What fantasies?" asked Thorn.

Greer paused, assessing whether or not to elaborate. He sat heavily in his chair, seeing Thorn's desperate eyes.

"For one thing, she fantasizes that her child is not really hers."

The statement crashed down upon Thorn like thunder. He sat paralyzed, unable to respond.

"I interpret this not so much as a fear, frankly, as a desire. She subconsciously wishes she were *childless*. This is a way of accomplishing that. At least on an emotional level."

Thorn was stunned, unable to reply.

"I don't mean to suggest that the child isn't important to her," continued Greer. "On the contrary, it's the single most important thing in her life. But for some reason it's very threatening to her. I don't really know if the fear revolves around motherhood, or emotional attachment, or simply the belief that she's inadequate. Unable to handle the job."

"But she *wanted* a child," Thorn managed to say.

"For you."

"No . . ."

"Subconsciously. She felt she needed to prove herself worthy of you. How better to do that than by bearing your child?"

Thorn gazed straight ahead, his eyes filled with despair.

"Now she finds she can't cope," continued Greer, "so she searches for a reason that won't make her feel inadequate. She fantasizes that the child isn't hers, that the child is evil . . ."

". . . What?"

"She's unable to love it," explained Greer, "so she invents a reason why it's not worthy of her love."

"She thinks the child is evil?"

Thorn was shaken now, his face rigid with fear.

"It's necessary right now for her to feel this way," explained Greer. "But the point is that, at this time, another child would be disastrous."

"In what way . . . 'evil'?"

"This is just a fantasy. Just like the fantasy that the child isn't hers."

Thorn drew in his breath, fighting back a wave of nausea.

"There's no need to despair," assured Greer.

"Doctor . . ."

"Yes?"

Thorn was unable to continue; the two sat in silence, gazing at one another across the vast room.

"You were about to say something?" asked Greer.

The doctor's face registered concern, for the man before him was plainly afraid to speak.

"Mr. Thorn? Are you all right?"

"I'm frightened," Thorn whispered.

"Of course you're frightened."

"I mean . . . I'm afraid."

"This is natural."

"Something . . . terrible is happening."

"Yes. But you'll both live through it."

"You don't understand."

"I do."

"No."

"Believe me. I do."

Thorn, near tears, lowered his head into his hands.

"You've been under a strain, Mr. Thorn. Obviously more than you know."

"I don't know what to do," Thorn moaned.

"Number one, you should agree to an abortion."

Thorn raised his eyes, firmly meeting Greer's.

"No," he said. The psychiatrist reacted with surprise.

"If it's your religious principles . . ."

"No."

"Surely you can see the need . . ."

"I won't do it," said Thorn resolutely.

"You must."

"No."

Greer leaned back in his chair, regarding the Ambassador with dismay.

"I'd like to know your reason," he said quietly.

Thorn gazed at him unmoving.

"It was foretold that this pregnancy would be terminated," he said, "and I'm going to fight to see that it's not."

The doctor stared at him, puzzled and concerned.

"I know what this must sound like," said Thorn. "And maybe I am . . . *insane*."

"Why do you say that?"

Thorn looked hard at him and spoke through a taut jaw.

"Because this pregnancy must endure to keep me from believing."

"Believing . . . ?"

"As my wife does. That the child is . . ."

The word stuck in his throat, and he rose, filled with a sense of urgency. A premonition had swept over him. He feared that something was about to happen.

"Mr. Thorn?"

"Forgive me . . ."

"Please sit down."

With an abrupt shake of his head, Thorn exited, heading quickly for the stairs that would take him outside. Once on the street, he moved at a run, a sense of panic welling within him as he made it to his car, fumbling with his keys. There was something wrong. He needed to be home. Flooring the accelerator, he swung a fast U-turn, tires squealing as he headed back in the direction of the highway. Pereford was a half hour away and he feared, though he didn't know why, that he might not get there in time. The streets of London were filled with midday traffic; he sounded his horn, swerving and running stoplights as the sense of desperation overwhelmed him.

At Pereford House, Katherine felt the anxiety too, busying herself with household duties in an attempt to quiet her gnawing fear. She stood now on the second-floor landing, pitcher in hand, wondering how to reach the plants that hung suspended just over the railing. She wanted to water them, but feared spilling the water onto the tile floor two stories below. Behind her, in his playroom, Damien rode his wheeled car, making the sound of a freight train, a sound that intensified as he rode faster. Unseen by Katherine, Mrs. Baylock stood in a far corner of the child's room, her eyes closed, as though locked in prayer.

On the highway, the tires squealed harshly as Thorn

turned onto the cloverleaf that spewed the vehicle onto M-40, the direct road home. Thorn's face was taut with tension, his hands squeezing the wheel as the pavement blurred beneath him, his body straining with every fiber to urge the car forward. It zipped down the highway like a streak of beige lightning, passing other cars as though they were standing still. Thorn was perspiring now, as each car ahead of him became a target to be overtaken. He blasted his horn, and each car made way as his car shot ahead. He thought of the police and glanced in the rear-view mirror. And there he saw the ominous shape moving up behind him. It was another car, black and massive, following his every move. The car was a hearse. And it was gaining on him. And as Thorn watched it coming up from behind, his face froze with fear.

At Pereford, Damien sped faster on his toy car, pounding up on it as though it were a racehorse. In the hallway, Katherine stepped up onto a stool. In Damien's room, Mrs. Baylock gazed hard at the child as if directing him with the sheer force of willpower to go faster and the boy accelerated, wild-eyed, his face filled with frenzy.

Within his car, Thorn groaned with exertion, pushing the accelerator into the floor. The hearse was gaining on him, the face of the driver gazing coldly, directly ahead. Thorn's speedometer registered ninety, then rose to a hundred and ten, but the hearse kept coming, moving doggedly ahead. Thorn was panting now and he knew his reasoning had left him, but he was powerless to stop. He could not be overtaken. The machinery of his car screamed beneath him, but the hearse kept coming, moving up alongside.

"No . . ." Thorn moaned, "no . . . . !"

And then they flew neck and neck, the hearse continuing to gain. Thorn pounded his wheel, demanding his car move faster, but the hearse was overtaking him, a coffin in the back moving slowly by.

In the Thorn house, Damien accelerated faster, his toy car careening wildly as it hurtled about the room, while outside in the hallway Katherine reached up tentatively from her perch on the stool.

On the highway, the hearse suddenly pulled farther ahead, as Thorn let out a bloodcurdling cry. And in that instant Damien shot out of his room, his toy car colliding with Katherine, sending her flying from her stool, clawing air as she toppled into space. Hurtling backward, she cried out, desperately grabbing for the balcony railing, taking with her a circular goldfish bowl that tumbled down beside her. Her scream ended with a sudden impact, the goldfish bowl hitting a second later and exploding into glistening shards.

Katherine lay silent now, and still; a delicate goldfish flopped on the cold tile next to her.

By the time Thorn got to the hospital, the reporters were already there, shouting questions and popping flashbulbs in his eyes as he desperately pushed his way through to a door marked INTENSIVE CARE. He'd arrived home to find Mrs. Baylock in a state of hysterics; she told him only that Katherine had had a fall and was taken by ambulance to City Hospital.

"Any word on her condition, Mr. Thorn?" shouted a reporter.

"Get out of my way."

"They say she had a fall."

"Let me through."

"Is she all right?"

He made his way through a double door, the reporters' voices fading behind as he ran down the hall.

"Ambassador Thorn?"

"Yes."

A doctor appeared, quickly walking toward him.

"My name is Becker," he said.

"Is she all right?" Thorn asked desperately.

"She'll recover. She hit pretty hard. She has a concussion, a broken collarbone, and some internal bleeding."

"She's pregnant."

"I'm afraid not."

"She lost it?" he gasped.

"On the floor where she hit. I was going to make an examination, but apparently your maid cleaned everything up by the time we got there."

Thorn shuddered and sagged against the wall.

"Naturally," continued the doctor, "we'll keep the details of how it happened quiet. The less people know the better."

Thorn stared at him, and the doctor saw he was confused.

"You *do* know she jumped," he said.

". . . Jumped?"

"From your second-floor balcony. Apparently in full view of your child and his nanny."

Thorn merely stared at him. Then he turned his face to the wall. From the tensing of his shoulders the doctor could tell he was crying.

"In a fall like this," added the doctor, "it's usually the head that hits first. So in a sense you can consider yourself lucky."

Thorn nodded, trying to stop his tears.

"There's no need for that," said the doctor. "There's a lot to be grateful for. She's still alive, and with the proper care she probably won't ever try it again. My own sister-in-law was suicidal. Took a bath and brought the toaster into it. When she pushed down the handle, she electrocuted herself."

Thorn turned and gazed at him.

"Point is, she lived through it and never tried it again. It's been four years now and no trouble at all."

"Where is she?" asked Thorn.

"She lives in Switzerland."

"My wife."

"Room 4A. She should be coming around soon."

Katherine's room was quiet and dark; a nurse was seated in the corner with a magazine as Thorn entered and stopped, his face filled with shock. The sight of Katherine was awesome. Her face was swollen and discolored; a tube from her arm led upward to a bottle of plasma. Her arm was in a cast, grotesquely crooked; she seemed unconscious, her face devoid of life.

"She's sleeping," the nurse said. Thorn moved stiffly forward to her bed. As though sensing his presence, Katherine moaned and slowly moved her head.

"Is she in pain?" Thorn asked in a shaking voice.

"She's on cloud nine," answered the nurse. "Sodium pentothal."

Thorn sat beside her, leaned his forehead on her bed, and wept. After a time he was aware that Katherine's hand had touched his head.

"Jerry . . ." she whispered.

He looked up to see her struggling to open her eyes.

"Kathy . . ." he moaned through his tears.

"Don't let him kill me."

And then she closed her eyes and slept.

Thorn arrived home after midnight and stood for a long time in the darkness of the downstairs foyer, gazing at the spot on the tile floor where Katherine had landed. He felt numb, his body racked with exhaustion, and he longed for sleep, anything to wipe out the tragedy of what had occurred. Their life had changed now, unalterably; it was as though they were under a curse.

Thorn flicked out the downstairs lights and stood for a time in the darkness, his eyes finding their way to the landing at the top of the stairs. He tried to imagine Katherine there, contemplating the jump. Why, if she were serious about ending her life, had she not chosen the roof? There were pills in the house, there were razor blades, a dozen other likely implements or ways to end it. Why this? And why in front of Damien and Mrs. Baylock?

He thought again of the priest and his warning. "He will kill the unborn child while it slumbers in the womb. Then he will kill your wife. Then when he is certain to inherit all that is yours . . ." He closed his eyes, trying to force it out of his mind. He thought of Tassone, dead on the pole, of the phone call from Jennings, of his unreasoning panic as the hearse overtook him on the highway. The psychiatrist was right. He was under a strain and his behavior proved it. Katherine's fears had spread to him; her fantasies were somehow contagious. He could no longer allow it to happen. Now more than ever, he must be clear and rational.

Feeling physically weak, he moved to the stairs, climbing upward in darkness. He would sleep and in the morning awake refreshed, with renewed energy, able to deal with things.

Reaching the door to his own room, he paused, gazing down the darkened hall toward Damien's. The soft glow of the nightlight spilled outward from beneath the door. Thorn imagined the child's face in the peaceful innocence of slumber. Longing to see him he moved slowly toward Damien's room, seeking reassurance that there was nothing to fear. But as he cracked open the child's door, he came upon a scene that made him shudder. The child was asleep, but he was not alone. One one side sat Mrs. Baylock, her arms folded as she gazed resolutely into space, and on the other side was the massive form of a dog. It was the dog he had told her to get rid of, but it was back now, sitting at attention, as though standing guard over the sleeping form of his son. With his breath coming shallow, Thorn silently closed the door and backed down the hall until he made it to his room. He stood there, trying to quiet his breath, aware he was shaking. Suddenly the silence was shattered. A phone was ringing, and he raced to his bedside to pick it up.

"Hello . . ."

"It's Jennings," a voice said. "You know, the one whose camera you busted?"

"Yes."

"I'm at the corner of Grosvernor and Fifth in Chelsea, and I think you better meet me here right away."

"What do you want?"

"Something's happening, Mr. Thorn. Something's happening that you ought to know."

Jennings' apartment was in a slum district and Thorn had trouble finding it. It was raining, the visibility poor, and he was about to give up when he spotted the infrared glow high in a turret above the street. Jennings was in the window and waved to him, then turned, realizing he should have cleaned up before being visited by such a distinguished guest. He kicked some clothes into a closet and smoothed the blanket on his bed, then opened the door and waited for Thorn. The Ambassador appeared out of breath, from the walk up five flights of stairs.

"I've got some brandy if you like."

"Please."

"Not the kind you're accustomed to, I'm sure."

Jennings closed the door and disappeared into an alcove, as Thorn's eyes scanned the darkened room. It was bathed in a reddish glow that came from the opened door of a closet-sized darkroom, the walls adorned with blown-up photos.

"Here we go," Jennings said, returning with a bottle and glasses. "Little of this and you'll be ready for the Turks."

Thorn accepted his glass and Jennings poured; Jennings then sat on the bed, gesturing toward a pile of pillows on the floor, but Thorn remained standing.

"Cheers," said Jennings. "Care for a smoke?"

Thorn shook his head, unnerved by the man's casual mood.

"You said something was happening."

"That it is."

"I'd like to know what you meant."

Jennings studied him carefully.

"Don't you know already?"

"No, I don't."

"Then why are you here?"

"You wouldn't explain yourself on the phone."

Jennings nodded and put down his glass.

"I couldn't explain it because it's something you've got to see."

"What is it?"

"It's photos." He rose and entered the darkroom, gesturing Thorn to follow. "I thought you might want to be sociable first."

"I'm very tired."

"Well, this will get your heart beating."

He turned on a small lamp, spotlighting a group of photos; Thorn entered and sat on a stool beside Jennings.

"Recognize these?"

They were pictures of the party. Damien's fourth birthday party; shots of children riding the carousel, shots of Katherine gazing into the crowd.

"Yes," replied Thorn.

"Take a look at this one."

Jennings removed the top photos, revealing one of Chessa, Damien's first nanny. She was standing alone in her clown costume, framed against the background of the house.

"See anything unusual?" asked Jennings.

"No."

Jennings touched the photo, tracing with his finger the vague haze that hung about her neck and head.

"Thought it was a blemish at first," said Jennings. "But look how it works with the next one."

126

He pulled out a photo of Chessa, hanging from the roof.

"I don't understand," said Thorn.

"Bear with me."

Jennings moved aside the stack of photos, replacing it with another. On top was a shot of the small priest, Tassone, walking away from the Embassy.

"How 'bout that one?"

Thorn turned to him with dismay.

"Where did you get this?"

"Took it."

"I thought you were *looking* for this man. You said you were related to him."

"I lied. Just look at the picture."

Jennings touched the photo, pointing out the hazy appendage that seemed to hang over the priest's head.

"That 'shadow' over his head?" asked Thorn.

"Yes. Then look at this one. Taken about ten days later."

He shuffled to another photo and put it under the light. It was a blow-up of a group of people standing at the back of an auditorium. Tassone's face could not be seen, only priestly robes, but just above where the head should have been was the same oblong shape hanging in the air.

"I figure it's the same man. You can't see his face, but you can see what's hanging above him."

Thorn studied the picture, his eyes filled with confusion.

"It's a little more pronounced this time," continued Jennings. "If you envision the size of his face, you can see it's just about making contact with his head. In the ten days between the first picture and this one, it moved down. Whatever it is, it came closer."

Thorn stared, dumfounded; Jennings removed the photo and replaced it with the one carried on the front page of the newspapers; the priest impaled on the spearlike pole.

"Begin to see the connection?" asked Jennings.

Thorn sat stunned. Behind them an automatic timer went off and Jennings flicked on another light, turning to meet Thorn's troubled gaze.

"I can't explain it either," said Jennings. "That's why I started digging."

Taking a pair of tongs, he turned to a vat, lifting out an enlargement, waving and letting it drip before moving it to the light.

"I've got some friends at the police. They gave me some negatives that I made enlargements from. The coroner's report showed he was riddled with cancer. High on morphine most of the time, injected himself two, three times a day."

As Thorn's eyes fell on the enlargements, he winced. It was in three separate panels, each a different death pose of the priest's naked body.

"Externally, his body was completely normal," continued Jennings. "Except for one small item on the inside of his left thigh."

He handed Thorn a magnifying glass, guiding his hand to the last panel. It was of the priest grotesquely spread-eagled, his genitals and thighs exposed to view. Thorn looked closely, seeing the mark. It looked somewhat like a tattoo.

"What is it?" asked Thorn.

"Three sixes. Six hundred sixty-six."

". . . Concentration camp?"

"That was my thought, but a biopsy showed it was literally carved into him. They didn't do that in the concentration camps. This was self-inflicted, I'd suppose."

Thorn and Jennings exchanged a glance, Thorn completely at a loss.

"Bear with me," said Jennings, and he lifted another photo to the light. "This is the room where he lived. Cold-water flat in Soho. Filled with rats when we entered. He'd left a salt-beef half-eaten on the table."

Thorn examined the photo. It showed a small cubicle with only a table, a bureau, and a bed. The walls were covered with a strange texture, like crumpled scraps of paper; large crosses were hanging everywhere.

"The whole place looked like this. The papers all over the walls are pages from the Bible. Thousands of them. Every inch of wall space was covered with them, even the windows. As though he was trying to keep something out."

Thorn sat stunned, gazing at the bizarre photograph.

"Crosses, too. There were forty-seven of them nailed to the front door alone."

"He was . . . crazy . . .? Thorn whispered.

Jennings looked him directly in the eye.

"You know better than that."

Jennings swiveled in his chair and opened a drawer, producing a tattered folder.

"The police dismissed him as a kook," he said. "Let me rummage through and take what I wanted. That's how I got this."

Jennings rose and moved into the living room, Thorn following. There the photographer upended the folder, spilling its contents onto the table.

"The first item is a diary," he said, lifting a small tattered book from the pile. "It doesn't tell about *him*, it tells about *you*. *Your* movements. When you left your office, where you went, what restaurants you had lunch in, where your speaking engagements were . . ."

"May I see it?"

"Be my guest."

Thorn took it with trembling hands and slowly leafed through the pages.

"The last notation says you were scheduled to meet with *him*," continued Jennings. "In Kew Gardens. That's dated the same day he died. Seems to me the police might have taken a little more interest if they had known that."

Thorn raised his eyes, and they locked with Jennings'.

"He was insane," said Thorn.

"Was he?"

Jennings' tone was threatening, and Thorn stiffened under his gaze.

"What do you want?"

"Did you meet with him?"

"No."

"I've got more information yet to come, Mr. Ambassador, but it won't come unless you tell me the truth."

"What's your interest in this?" Thorn hissed under his breath.

"I want to be of service," answered Jennings. "I'm your friend."

Thorn remained rigid, his eyes fixed on Jennings.

"The really important items are here," said Jennings, pointing to the table. "You want to talk, or do you want to walk out?"

Thorn gritted his teeth.

"What do you want to know?"

"Did you see him in the park?"

"Yes."

"What did he say?"

"He warned me."

"About what?"

"He said my life was in danger."

"What kind of danger?"

"He wasn't clear."

"Don't bullshit me."

"I'm not. He wasn't making sense."

Jennings stepped back, eyeing Thorn with doubt.

"It was about the Bible," Thorn added. "It was a poem. I don't remember it. I thought he was insane. I couldn't understand it, I'm telling you the truth. I don't remember it, and I couldn't understand it!"

Jennings seemed skeptical as Thorn fidgeted under his gaze.

"I think you should confide in me," said Jennings.

"You said you had more information."

"Not until I hear more."

"I have nothing more to say."

Jennings nodded in surrender and sifted through the items on the table. Flicking on a bare bulb suspended overhead, he found a newspaper clipping and handed it to Thorn.

"It's from a magazine called *Astrologer's Monthly*. A report by an astologer of what he calls an 'unusual phenomenon.' A comet that took the shape of a glowing star. Like the star of Bethlehem, two thousand years ago."

Thorn studied the article, wiping the perspiration that formed on his upper lip.

"Only *this* one happened on the *other* side of the world," Jennings continued. "The European continent. Just four years ago. *June sixth* to be exact. Does that date ring a bell?"

"Yes," answered Thorn hoarsely.

"Then you'll recognize this second clipping," replied Jennings, lifting another scrap from the pile. "It's from the back page of a newspaper in Rome."

Thorn took it from him, recognizing it immediately. Katherine had it in a scrapbook at home.

"It's the birth announcement of your son. That was *also* June sixth, four years ago. I'd call that a coincidence, wouldn't you?"

Thorn's hands were trembling now; the papers fluttering so he could barely read.

"Was your son born at six A.M.?"

Thorn turned to him, his eyes filled with anguish.

"I'm trying to figure out the mark on the priest's thigh. The three sixes. I think it relates to your son. The sixth month, the sixth day . . ."

"My son is *dead*," blurted Thorn. "My son is *dead*. I don't know whose son I'm raising!"

He raised his hands to his head and turned toward

the darkness, his breath coming heavily as Jennings watched him.

"If you wouldn't mind, Mr. Thorn," said Jennings quietly, "I'd like to help you find out."

"No," Thorn groaned. "This is *my* problem."

"You're wrong, sir," replied Jennings sadly. "It's my problem, too."

Thorn turned to him and their eyes held. Jennings slowly moved into the darkroom and reappeared with a final photograph in his hand. He handed it over to Thorn.

"There was a small mirror in the corner of the priest's room," Jennings said with difficulty. "Happened to catch my own reflection in it when I took one of the pictures."

Thorn's eyes moved to the photo, his face registering his shock.

"Rather unusual effect," Jennings said. "Don't you think?"

He swung the bare bulb closer to Thorn so he could see more clearly. There, in the photograph of Tassone's room, was a small mirror in a far corner, reflecting Jennings with the camera poised in front of his face. There was nothing unusual about a photographer catching his own reflection in a mirror, but in this case there was something missing. It was Jennings' neck, the head separated by a blemish of haze from his body.

Chapter Ten

On the following morning the news of Katherine's injury made it easy for Thorn to excuse himself from the office for the next few days. He told his staff he was going to Rome to find a bone specialist on Katherine's behalf; in truth, he was going on a different kind of mission. Having told the whole story to the photographer, he had been convinced by Jennings to start at the beginning, to return to the hospital where Damien was born. There they would begin putting together the pieces.

The trip was arranged quickly, without fanfare, Thorn hiring a private jet in order to depart from London and arrive in Rome on runways blocked to public access. In the hours before their departure, Jennings busied himself in gathering research material: several versions of the Bible, three books on the occult. Thorn returned to Pereford to pack his bags, including a hat to mask his identity.

At Pereford, things were unusually quiet. As Thorn wandered through the empty house, he realized that Mrs. Horton was nowhere about. Her husband, too; the cars, were parked side by side in the garage with a certain finality.

"They're both gone," Mrs. Baylock said as Thorn entered the kitchen.

The woman was working over the sink, cutting vegetables, in the way that Mrs. Horton had always done.

"Gone out?" asked Thorn.

"Gone. Just up and quit. They left an address for you to send their last month's wages."

Thorn was shocked.

"Did they say why?" he asked.

"No matter, sir. I can carry on."

"They must have given a reason."

"Not to me, they didn't. But they didn't speak to me much, anyway. It was the man who insisted on going. I think Mrs. Horton wanted to stay."

Thorn gazed at her with troubled eyes. It frightened him to leave her alone in the house with Damien. But there was no remedy for it. He had to go.

"Can you carry on here if I leave for a few days?"

"I think so, sir. We've got enough groceries for a couple of weeks, and I think the boy will appreciate the peace and quiet in the house."

Thorn nodded and started to leave.

"Mrs. Baylock?" he asked.

"Sir?"

"That dog."

"Oh, I know, it'll be gone by the end of the day."

"Why is it still here?"

"We took it out to the country and let it go and it found its way back. It was at the door last night after . . . well, after the 'accident,' and the boy was pretty shook up and he asked if it could stay in his room. I told him you wouldn't like it, but under the circumstances I thought . . ."

"I want it out of here."

"Yes, sir. I'll call the Humane Society today."

Thorn turned to go.

"Mr. Thorn?"

"Yes?"

"How's the wife?"

"She's doing well."

"While you're gone, could I take the boy to see her?"

Thorn paused, studying the woman as she grabbed a kitchen towel and began drying her hands. She was the very picture of domesticity and he was suddenly confused as to why he so disliked her.

"I'd rather you didn't. I'll take him when I get back."

"Very good, sir."

They nodded to one another and Thorn left, driving his own car to the hospital. There he consulted with Dr. Becker who informed him that Katherine was awake and feeling relaxed. He asked if he might have a psychiatrist visit her and Thorn gave him the number of Charles Greer. He then went into Katherine's room, and she smiled weakly when she saw him.

"Hi," he said.

"Hi," she whispered.

"Feeling better?"

"Some."

"They say you're going to be fine."

"I'm sure."

Thorn pulled up a chair and sat beside her. He was struck with her beauty, even in this condition; the sunlight streamed in through the window, gently illuminating her hair.

"You look nice," she said.

"I was thinking about you," he replied.

"I'm sure I'm a vision," she smiled.

He took her hand and held it; both gazing into each other's eyes.

"Strange times," she said softly.

"Yes."

"Is it ever going to be all right?"

"I think so."

She smiled sadly, and he reached up, brushing a wisp of hair from her eyes.

"We're good people, aren't we, Jeremy?" she asked.

"I think so."

"Then why is everything going wrong?"

He shook his head, unable to answer.

"If we were terrible people," she said quietly, "then I'd say 'Okay.' Maybe this is what we deserve. But what did we do wrong? What did we ever do wrong?"

"I don't know," he whispered hoarsely.

She seemed so vulnerable and innocent, and he was flooded with emotion.

"You'll be safe here," he whispered. "I'm going away for a few days."

She had no reaction. She didn't even ask him where.

"It's business," he said. "Something I can't avoid."

"How long?"

"Three days. I'll call you every day."

She nodded, and he slowly rose, leaning over to gently kiss her bruised, discolored cheek.

"Jerry?"

"Hm?"

"They tell me I jumped."

She gazed up at him, her eyes puzzled and childlike.

"Is that what they told *you*?" she asked.

"Yes."

"Why should I do that?"

"I don't know," whispered Thorn. "That's what we'll have to find out."

"Am I crazy?" she asked simply.

Thorn gazed at her, then slowly shook his head.

"Maybe we all are," he replied.

She reached up and he leaned down again, bringing his face close to hers.

"I didn't jump," she whispered. "Damien pushed me."

There passed a long silence, and Thorn slowly left the room.

The six-seat Lear Jet was empty save for Thorn and Jennings, and as it streaked through the darkened skies toward Rome, the atmosphere within was silent and tense. Jennings had his research books spread out around him and prodded Thorn to remember everything Tassone had told him.

"I can't," said Thorn with anguish. "It's all a blur."

"Start at the beginning. Tell me everything you can."

Thorn recounted his first meeting with the priest, how the priest followed him, finally cornering him and soliciting the meeting in the park. It was at that meeting, the second that he had recited the poem.

"Something about . . . rising from the sea . . ." Thorn mumbled as he struggled to recall. ". . . About death . . . and armies . . . the Roman Empire . . ."

"You've got to do better than that."

"I was upset. I thought he was crazy! I didn't really listen."

"But you *did* listen. You *heard*. You've got the key to this, now spit it up!"

"I can't!"

"Try harder."

Thorn's face was filled with frustration and he shut his eyes, forcing his mind in a direction it refused to take.

"I remember . . . he begged me to take communion. Drink the blood of Christ. That's what he said. Drink the blood of Christ . . ."

"What for?"

"To defeat the son of the Devil. He said drink the blood of Christ to defeat the son of the Devil."

"What else?" urged Jennings.

"An old man. Something about an old man . . ."

"What old man?"

"He said I should see an old man."

"Keep going . . ."

"I can't remember . . . !"

"Did he give you a name?"

"M . . . Magdo. Magdo. Meggido. No, that was the town."

"What town?" pressed Jennings.

"The town he said I should go to. *Meggido*. I'm sure that's it. That's where he said I should go."

Jennings excitedly rummaged through his briefcase, retrieving a map.

"Meggido . . ." he mumbled, "Meggido . . ."

"Have you heard of it?" asked Thorn.

"I'll just bet it's in Italy."

But it was not. Nor was it to be found listed in any country on the greater European continent. Jennings studied his map for a full half hour before closing it and shaking his head with dismay. He glanced at Thorn and saw that the Ambassador had fallen asleep. He did not wake him, turning instead to his books on the occult. As the small plane knifed through the midnight sky, he became absorbed in the prophesies of the second coming of Christ. It was linked with the coming of the Anti-Christ, the Unholy Child, the Beast, the Savage Messiah:

> . . . and unto this earth comes the Savage Messiah, the offspring of Satan in human form, sired by the rape of a four-legged beast. As young Christ spread love and kindness, so the Anti-Christ will spread hatred and fear . . . receiving his commandments directly from Hell.

The plane touched down with a jolt. Jennings grabbed for his books as they fell in disarray around him. It was raining in Rome, the thunder rumbling ominously above them.

Moving quickly through the empty airport, they made it to a waiting cab; Jennings catnapped as they moved slowly through a downpour toward the other side of the city. Thorn sat in numbed silence as they passed the lighted statuary of the Via Veneto, remembering how he and Katherine, once young and full of hope, wandered hand in hand down these very streets. They were innocent and in love; he remembered the smell of her perfume and the sound of her laughter. They discovered Rome in the way that Columbus discovered America. They claimed it as their own. They made love in the afternoon here. Now, as Thorn gazed into the night, he wondered if they would make love ever again.

"Ospedale Generale," said the cabdriver as he came to an abrupt stop.

Jennings awoke and Thorn squinted out into the night, his face filled with confusion.

"This isn't it," Thorn said.

"*Si.* Ospedale Generale."

"No, it was old. Brick. I remember."

"Is it the right address?" asked Jennings.

"Ospedale Generale," the driver repeated.

"*È differente,*" insisted Thorn.

"Ah," replied the driver. "*Fuoco. Tre anni più o meno.*"

"What's he say?" asked Jennings.

"Fire," replied Thorn. "*Fuoco* is fire."

"*Si,*" added the driver. "*Tre anni.*"

"What about fire?" asked Jennings.

"Apparently the old hospital burned down. It's been rebuilt."

"*Tre anni più or meno. Multo morte.*"

Thorn glanced at Jennings.

"Three years ago. *Multo morte.* Much death."

They paid the cabdriver and asked him to wait. He refused at first, but then, seeing the kind of money they shoved at him, he readily agreed. Thorn told him in broken Italian that they would like to keep him with them until they left Rome. The driver wanted to go call his wife, but promised to return.

Inside the hospital, they were immediately frustrated. As it was quite late, the people in charge would not be returning until morning. Jennings moved off on his own, seeking someone in authority while Thorn found an English-speaking nun who confirmed that the fire three years ago had reduced the building to ruins.

"Surely it didn't destroy *everything*," Thorn entreated. "There must be some records . . ."

"I was not here," she replied in broken English. "But they say it took everything."

"Is it possible that some of the papers were stored elsewhere?"

"I do not know."

Thorn grimaced with frustration as the nun shrugged, unable to offer more.

"Look," Thorn said. "This is very important to me. I adopted a child here, and I'm looking for some record of its birth."

"There were no adoptions here."

"There was *one*. It wasn't an actual adoption."

"You are mistaken. Our adoptions are done through the relief agency."

"Are there birth records? Do you keep records somewhere of the children born here?"

"Yes, of course."

"Maybe if I gave you a date——"

"It's no use," interrupted Jennings.

Thorn turned to see him approaching, his expression set in despair.

"The fire started in the Hall of Records. In the basement. All the paperwork was there; it went up like a torch. Shot up the stairwells . . . the third floor became an inferno."

"Third floor . . . ?"

"Nursery and maternity ward," nodded Jennings. "Nothing left but ashes."

Thorn sagged, leaning heavily against a wall.

"If you'll excuse me . . ." said the nun.

"Wait." begged Thorn. What about the staff? Surely *some* survived."

"Yes. Some."

"There was a tall man. A priest. A giant of a man."

"Was his name Spilletto?"

"Yes," replied Thorn excitedly. "Spilletto."

"He was chief of staff," replied the nun.

"Yes. He was in charge. Is he . . ."

"He lived."

Thorn's heart surged with hope. "Is he here?"

"No."

"Where?"

"A monastery in Subiaco. Many of the survivors were taken there. Many died there. He might have died. But he lived through the fire. I remember they said it was a miracle he survived. He was on the third floor at the time of the fire."

"Subiaco?" asked Jennings.

The nun nodded. "The Monastery of San Benedetto."

Racing to the cab, they poured over Jennings' maps. Subiaco was on the southern border of Italy; to reach it they would have to drive through the night. The cab-driver complained, but they gave him more money, tracing the route in red pencil so he could follow it while they slept. But they were too keyed up to sleep; instead they turned to Jennings' books, studying them under the dim interior light as the small cab sped through the Italian countryside.

"I'll be damned . . ." whispered Jennings, as he gazed down into a Bible. "Here we go."

"What is it?"

"It's all right here in the Bible. In the bloody Book of Revelations. When the Jews return to Zion——"

"That was it," interrupted Thorn excitedly. "The poem. When the Jews return to Zion. Then something about a comet . . ."

"That's here too," said Jennings, pointing to another book. "A shower of stars, and the rise of the Holy Roman Empire. These are supposed to be the events that signal the birth of the Anti-Christ. The Devil's own child."

As the cab pressed onward, they continued to read, Thorn pulling from his briefcase the interpretive text he'd once used to prepare a speech in which he quoted

141

from the Bible. It provided the clarity they needed to make sense of the symbols in the scriptures.

"So the Jews *have* returned to Zion," concluded Jennings as morning neared, "and there *has* been a comet. And as for the rise of the Holy Roman Empire, scholars think that could well be interpreted as the formation of the Common Market."

"Bit of a stretch . . ." Thorn pondered.

"Then how 'bout this?" asked Jennings, opening one of his books. "Revelations says: 'He will come forth from the Eternal Sea.' "

"That's the poem again. Tassone's poem." Thorn squinted trying to recall. "From the Eternal Sea He rises . . . with armies on either shore. That's how it began."

"He was quoting Revelations all the way. The poem was taken from the Book of Revelations."

"From the Eternal Sea He rises . . ." Thorn fought to remember more.

"Here's the point, Thorn," said Jennings, pointing to his book. "It says that the Caucus of International Theological Sciences has interpreted the 'Eternal Sea' to mean the world of *politics*. The Sea that constantly rages with the turmoil and revolution."

Jennings gazed hard into Thorn's eyes.

"The Devil's child will rise from the world of politics," he declared.

Thorn did not respond, his eyes turning toward the slowly brightening landscape.

The Monastery of San Benedetto was in a state of semidecay, but the massive fortress made of stone retained its strength and dignity even as the elements began to reclaim it. It had stood on its mountain in the southern Italian countryside for centuries and had withstood many sieges. At the outset of World War II, all the monks within were shot by invading German forces who used it as their headquarters. In 1946 it was mortared by the Italians themselves, as retribution for the evil work that had gone on within.

Yet for all of the earthly onslaughts upon it, San Benedetto was a holy place; stark and gothic upon its hill, the sound of religious prayer had echoed off its walls throughout the centuries, rising upward from the very vaults of history.

As the small mud-splattered cab pulled up the road along its half-mile frontage the occupants within were asleep; the cabdriver had to reach back and jostle them into wakefulness.

"Signori?"

As Thorn stirred, Jennings lowered his window and breathed the morning air, gazing across the fresh and dampened landscape.

"San Benedetto," mumbled the weary driver.

Thorn rubbed his eyes, focusing on the starkly silhouetted monastery framed against an angry reddish morning sky.

"Just look at that . . ." whispered Jennings with awe.

"Can't we get any closer?" asked Thorn.

The driver shook his head.

"Apparently not," concluded Jennings.

Instructing the driver to pull over and get some sleep, they headed out on foot, and were soon waist-high in tall grass that soaked their pant-legs to the thigh. The going was rough and they were not dressed for it; their clothes bound them as they struggled across the field. Breathing hard in the overwhelming silence, Jennings paused and unsnapped his camera case, shooting off a half roll of pictures.

"Incredible," he whispered. "In-fucking-credible."

Thorn glanced back impatiently and Jennings hurried to catch up; together they walked forward, listening to their breath in the stillness, and to the distant sound of chanting that came, like a constant moan, from within.

"There's a lot of sadness here," said Jennings as

they reached the entranceway. "Just listen to it. Listen to the pain."

It was awesome; the monotonous chant seemed to emanate from the very walls of the stone corridors and archways, as they walked slowly inside, gazing around in the emptiness, attempting to trace the source of the prayer.

"This way, I think," Jennings said, pointing down a long corridor. "Look at the mud."

Ahead of them, the floor was marked with a path of brown discoloration. The movement of feet over the centuries had actually worn down the rock, creating a spillway where water flowed during times of heavy rains. It led toward a huge stone rotunda, sealed off by heavy wooden doors. As they slowly approached, the chant grew closer. Opening the doors, they gazed with awe at the sight before them. It was as though they had entered the Middle Ages, and the presence of God, of spiritual holiness, could be felt as though it were a physical, living thing. It was a huge and ancient room; stone steps led to a spacious altar on which stood a massive wooden cross, the figure of Christ upon it, chisled from stone. The rotunda itself was made of stone blocks laced with vines that joined at the center of a domed ceiling which opened at the top to the sky. At that hour, a shaft of light streamed down through it, illuminating the figure of Christ.

"This is what it's all about, man," whispered Jennings. "This is a place of worship."

Thorn nodded and his eyes scanned the chamber, coming to rest on a group of hooded monks, kneeling amid the benches as they prayed. The chant was emotional and unnerving; rising and falling, it seemed to renew itself each time it began to fade. Jennings unsnapped his light meter, trying to get a reading in the dimness of the chamber.

"Put that away," Thorn whispered.

"Should've brought my flash."

144

"I said put it away."

Jennings glared at Thorn, but obeyed. Thorn was deeply upset, his knees trembling as though insisting he kneel and pray.

"Are you all right?" Jennings whispered.

". . . I'm Catholic," Thorn replied in a quiet voice.

And then his face froze, his eyes riveted on something in the darkness. Jennings followed his gaze, and he saw it too. It was a wheelchair. And in it was the hulking figure of a man. Unlike the others, who were on their knees with heads bowed, the one in the wheelchair sat stiffly upright, his head tilted and arms bent as though paralyzed.

"Is that him?" whispered Jennings.

Thorn nodded; his eyes were wide with apprehension. They moved closer until they could see better; Jennings winced as the priest's features came into view. Half of his face was literally melted; the eye was opaque and stared blindly upward. The right hand was also grotesquely deformed, protruding from a sackcloth sleeve like a smooth, glistening stump.

"We don't know if he can see or hear," said the monk who stood over Spilletto in the monastery courtyard. "Since the fire he's not made a sound."

They were in what was once a garden, now fallen to decay and littered with broken statuary. The monk speaking had pushed Spilletto's wheelchair from the rotunda at the end of the services, and the two men had followed him, approaching only when they were out of earshot of the rest.

"He is fed and cared for by the brothers," the monk continued, "and we pray for his recovery when his penance is complete."

"Penance?" asked Thorn.

The monk nodded.

" 'Woe to the Shepherd who abandons his sheep.

May his right arm wither and his right eye lose its sight.' "

"He's fallen from grace?" asked Thorn.

"Yes."

"May I ask why?"

"For abandoning Christ."

Thorn and Jennings exchanged a quizzical glance.

"How do you know he's abandoned Christ?" Thorn asked of the monk.

"Confession."

"But he doesn't speak."

"Written confession. He has some movement of his left hand."

"What kind of confession?" pressed Thorn.

The monk paused, "May I ask the nature of your questions?"

"It's vitally important," replied Thorn earnestly. "I beg you to help us. There's a life at stake."

The monk studied Thorn's face and then nodded.

"Come with me."

Spilletto's cubicle was bare and boxlike, containing only a straw matress and a table made of stone. Like the rotunda, it had an open skylight that let light and rain in; a pool of water remained from the rains of the night before. Thorn noticed that the mattress was wet, and wondered if they all suffered such discomfort, or if this was part of Spilletto's private penance.

"It's drawn on the table," the monk said as they entered. "He wrote it out in coal."

Spilletto's wheelchair clattered as it crossed the uneven stones. They gathered around the small table, seeing the strange symbol the priest had drawn there.

"He did it when he first came here," the priest said. "We left the coal here on the table, but he has drawn no more."

It was a grotesque stick figure, etched unevenly in a childlike scrawl. It was bent and misshapen, its head surrounded with a semicircular line. What immediately

146

caught Jennings' eye were the three numerals surrounding the semicircle above the stick figure's head. They were sixes. Three of them. Like the mark on Tassone's thigh.

"You'll notice the curved line above the head," the monk said. "This indicates the hood of the monk. His own hood."

"It's a self-portrait?" asked Jennings.

"We believe so."

"What about the sixes?"

"Six is the sign of the Devil," the monk responded. "Seven is the perfect number, the number of Jesus. Six is the sign of Satan."

"Why three of them?" asked Jennings.

"We believe it signifies the Diabolical Trinity. The Devil, Anti-Christ, and False Prophet."

"Father, Son, and Holy Ghost," observed Thorn.

The monk nodded. "For everything holy, there is something unholy. This is the essence of temptation."

"Why do you consider this a confession?" asked Jennings.

"It is, as you say, a self-portrait. Or so we believe. It is surrounded, symbolically, by the triumvirate of Hell."

"So you don't know, specifically, the act to which he confesses?"

"The details are unimportant," replied the monk. "All that matters is that he wishes to repent."

Jennings and Thorn exchanged a long glance; Thorn's face was gripped with frustration.

"Can I talk to him?" Thorn asked.

"It will do no good."

Thorn glanced at Spilletto and shuddered at the sight of the glistening, frozen face.

"Father Spilletto," he said firmly, "my name is Thorn."

The priest stared mutely upward; unmoving, unhearing.

"It's no use," advised the monk.

But Thorn would not be stopped.

"Father Spilletto," Thorn repeated, "There was a *child*. I want to know where it's from."

"Please, Signor," entreated the monk.

"You confessed to *them!*" shouted Thorn. "Now confess to *me!* I want to know where that child is from!"

"I'll have to ask you to . . ."

"Father Spilletto! Hear me! Tell me!"

The monk attempted to reach Spilletto's chair, but Jennings blocked the way.

"Father Spilletto!" shouted Thorn into the mute, unmoving face. "I beg you! Where *is* she?! Who *was* she?! Please! Answer me *now!*"

And suddenly they were jarred, the very atmosphere thundering around them as bells in the church tower began to peal. It was ear-splitting; Thorn and Jennings shuddered as the sound rebounded off the stone monastery wall. Then Thorn looked down and saw it. The priest's hand was beginning to tremble and slowly rise.

"The coal!" shouted Thorn. "Give him the coal!"

Jennings' hand moved quickly, grabbing the lump of coal from the table and thrusting it into the trembling hand. As the bells continued to peal, the priest's hand jerked stiffly across the stone, forming crude letters that wavered with each impact of the deafening sound.

"It's a word!" exclaimed Jennings excitedly. "C . . . E . . . R . . ."

The priest was shaking in every fiber as he struggled to continue, the pain of exertion plain as his disfigured mouth stretched open, emitting an agonized animal-like moan.

"Keep going!" urged Thorn.

". . . V . . ." read Jennings, ". . . E . . . T . . ."

And suddenly the bells went silent; the priest dropped the coal from his spasmed fingers as his head fell back against the chair. Exhausted, his eyes gazed upward, his face bathed in sweat.

As the echo faded around them, they stood in silence, staring at the word scrawled out on the table.

". . . Cervet . . .?" asked Thorn.

"Cervet," echoed Jennings.

"Is that Italian?"

They turned to the monk who looked at the word, and then to Spilletto, with confusion in their eyes.

"Does that mean something to you?" asked Thorn.

"Cerveteri," the monk replied. "I think Cerveteri."

"What is it?" asked Jennings.

"It is an old cemetery. From Etruscan times. Cimitero di Sant'Angelo."

The stiffened body of the priest trembled again, and he moaned as though trying to speak. But then he fell silent, a relaxation settling over him as he surrendered to the overpowering limitations of his body.

Thorn and Jennings looked at the monk who shook his head with dismay.

"Cerveteri is nothing but ruins. The remains of the Shrine of Techulca."

"Techulca?" asked Jennings.

"The Etruscan devil-god. The Etruscans were devil worshippers. Their burial place was a sacrificial ground."

"Why would he write this?" asked Thorn.

"I do not know."

"Where is this place?" asked Jennings.

"There is nothing there, Signor, except graves . . . and a few wild hogs."

"Where is it?" repeated Jennings with insistence.

"Your cabdriver will know. Perhaps fifty kilometers north of Rome."

The cabdriver was hard to awaken; then Thorn and Jennings had to wait until he defecated in the field alongside the road. He was disgruntled now and sorry that he had taken the job, particularly when he heard

149

where they now wanted to go. Cerveteri was a place that God-fearing men avoided, and they would not reach it until after nightfall.

The storm that hung over Rome had spread outward, heavy rains slowing their progress as, in darkness, they swung off the main highway onto an older road that was washed out with mud and potholes. The cab faltered, its rear left wheel slipping into a trench, and they all had to get out and push. When they got back inside, they were drenched and shivering; Jennings checked his watch and noted it was close to midnight. It was the last thought he registered before falling asleep; awakening several hours later, he realized the cab was no longer moving, and all was silent within. Thorn was asleep beside him, wrapped in a blanket; all that could be seen of the driver were his mud-caked shoes as he lay snoring in the front seat.

Jennings fumbled with the door handle and moved stiffly into the night, staggering to a nearby stand of bushes to urinate. It was near dawn, the sky was beginning to show the first signs of light. Jennings blinked hard, trying to make out his surroundings. He slowly realized that they'd arrived at Cerveteri. Before him stood a spiked iron fence, and just beyond it, tombstones silhouetted against the faintly lightening sky.

He moved back to the cab and stared in at Thorn, then glanced at his watch. It was ten minutes to five. Walking quietly to the driver's door he reached in and removed the keys from the ignition, then went to the trunk, carefully unlocking it and lifting the lid. It rose with a squeal but the sound did not awaken the two within. Jennings rummaged in the darkness for his camera case and loaded a fresh roll of film. He then tested his flash attachment. It went off into his eyes, blinding him for a moment and causing him to stagger. He waited for his vision to clear, then hefted his equipment onto his shoulder, pausing as his eyes fell upon a tire iron nestled among oil-soaked rags in a corner of the trunk. He reached in and took it, tucking it into his belt, then slowly closed the lid and walked silently to the rusted iron fence. The ground was wet and Jennings was cold; he shivered as he moved along the fence, searching for a point of entry. There was none. Securing his equipment, he scaled the fence with the aid of a nearby tree, losing his footing for an instant and ripping his coat as he tumbled to the ground on the other side. Then, regaining his footing and adjusting his cameras, he headed off into the interior of the cemetery. The sky was getting lighter now and he could make out the details of the tombstones and crumbling statuary around him. They were elaborate and ornate, though disfigured with decay; gargoyle-like faces with broken expressions, crypts, some half collapsed, with rodents moving, unconcerned by his presence, in and out of the hollowed and darkened insides.

Though chilled, Jennings felt himself perspiring. He glanced about uneasily as he plodded forward through the heavy growth. He felt as though he were being watched; the vacant eyes of the gargoyles seemed to follow him as he passed. He paused, trying to quiet his uneasiness, and his eyes moved upward, riveted to what they saw. It was a giant stone idol staring down from above, its face frozen in anger, as though outraged by his trespass. Jennings' breath became shallow as he stared upward; the idol's bulging eyes seemed to demand that he retreat. Its face was human, its expression animal: a deeply furrowed forehead and bulbous nose, a gaping, fleshy mouth stretched open as though in rage. Jennings fought down a swell of fear and managed to raise his camera, snapping off three shots with his flash attachment, assaulting the stone face like a sudden stroke of lightning.

Within the cab Thorn's eyes slowly opened as he became aware that Jennings was gone. He moved out of the car, seeing the graveyard before him, its broken statuary now illuminated by the first rays of the dawn.

". . . Jennings . . . ?"

There was no reply. Thorn moved to the fence and called again. He was answered with a distant sound. It was the sound of movement within the graveyard, as though someone were walking toward him. Thorn gripped the slippery bars and, with effort, hefted himself over the fence, dropping heavily to the ground on the other side.

". . . Jennings?"

The sound of movement had ended. Thorn searched through the maze of broken statuary ahead. Forcing himself to move, he walked slowly forward, his shoes gurgling as they sank into mud. The half-headed gargoyles came into view, and Thorn was unnerved as he eyed them. There was a kind of stillness here that he had experienced before, a suspended silence as though the atmosphere itself were holding its breath. It was at Pereford that he had first felt it, the night he saw the eyes staring back from the forest. He paused now, fearing he was once again being watched. His eyes scanned the statuary, coming to rest on a massive cross planted upside down in the ground. He stiffened. From somewhere behind the cross came the sound. It was the sound of movement again, but this time it was coming fast, heading directly toward him. Thorn wanted to run but was rooted, his eyes widening as the sound crashed heavily down.

"Thorn!"

It was Jennings, breathless and wild-eyed as he exploded through a stand of bushes. Thorn's breath rushed out as he stood shaking; Jennings quickly moved forward with the tire iron grasped in his hand.

"I found it!" he gasped. "I found it!!"

"Found what?"

"Come here. Come with me!"

They moved at a run through the undergrowth,

Jennings dodging gravestones like a soldier running an obstacle course, Thorn struggling to keep up behind.

"There!" exclaimed Jennings as he stopped in a clearing. "Take a look. They're the ones!"

At his feet were two graves; dug close together, side by side. Unlike the others in the cemetery these were fairly recent; one full-sized, the other small, the headstones unadorned, bearing only names and dates.

"See the dates?" asked Jennings excitedly. "June sixth. *June sixth!* Four years ago. A mother and a child."

Thorn approached slowly and stood beside him, staring down at the mounds.

"They're the only recent ones in the whole place," said Jennings proudly. "The others are so old you can't even *read* them."

Unanswering, Thorn knelt, wiping dirt from the headstones to see what was inscribed.

". . . Maria Avedici Santora . . ." he read. "Bambino Santoya . . . In Morte et in Nate Amplexarantur Generationes."

"What does it mean?"

"It's Latin."

"What does it say?"

". . . In death . . . and birth . . . generations embrace."

"Quite a find, I'd say."

Jennings knelt beside Thorn, surprised to find his companion in tears. Thorn bowed his head and openly wept; Jennings waited for the tears to subside.

"This is it," Thorn moaned. "I know it. My child is buried here."

"And probably the woman who gave birth to the one you're raising."

Thorn looked into Jennings' eyes.

"Maria Santoya," said Jennings, pointing to the headstone. "There's a mother here and a child."

Thorn shook his head, trying to make sense of it.

"Look," said Jennings. "You demanded Spilletto tell you where the mother was. This is the mother. And this is probably your child."

"But why here? Why in this place?"

"I don't know."

"Why in this terrible place?"

Jennings watched Thorn, sharing his confusion.

"There's only one way to find out, Thorn. We've come all this way, we might as well do it."

He raised the tire iron, plunging it forcefully into the earth. It stopped with a dull thud, buried to the hilt.

"It's easy enough. They're only a foot or so under."

He began to dig with the tire iron, loosening the caked dirt and, with his hands, scraping it away.

"You going to help with this?" he asked Thorn, and Thorn reluctantly participated, his fingers numbed with cold as he clawed at the dirt.

Within half an hour they were covered with soot and perspiration, clearing the last bits of earth from two cement covers. They sat back on their knees and stared at them, assessing what had to be done next.

"Smell it?" asked Jennings.

"Yes."

"Must have been a hasty job. Not exactly up to health standards."

Thorn didn't respond; his face was gripped with anguish.

"Which one first?" asked Jennings.

"Do we need to do this?"

"Yes."

"It seems wrong."

"If you want, I'll go get the cabdriver."

Thorn gritted his teeth, then shook his head.

"Let's go then," said Jennings. "Do the big one first."

Jennings struck hard with his tire iron, wedging it against the side of the large cement lid. Then, with great effort, he pried it upward until he could get his fingers underneath.

"Come on, goddamnit!" he shouted at Thorn, and Thorn responded quickly, his arms shaking with exertion as he struggled with Jennings to raise the heavy lid.

"Weighs a bloody ton . . . !" Jennings groaned. As he threw his weight against it, the lid came up slowly; both of them strained with full force to hold it in place as their eyes searched the darkened chamber below.

"My God!" Jennings gasped.

It was the carcass of a jackal. Maggots and flies abounded in the decay, wriggling through bits of leathered flesh that somehow still clung to the bones.

His mouth flying open, Thorn lurched backward, the cement slipping from his grip and crashing downward, breaking into pieces in the crypt below. A horde of flies billowed upward; Jennings moved in sudden terror, slipping in mud, as he grabbed Thorn, trying to pull him away.

"No!!" cried Thorn.

"Let's go!"

"No!" gasped Thorn. "The *other* one!"

"What for? We've seen what we need!"

"No, the *other* one," Thorn moaned desperately. "Maybe it's an animal, too!"

"So what?!"

"Then maybe my child's *alive* somewhere!"

Jennings paused, held by the agony in Thorn's eyes. Quickly retrieving the tire iron, he jammed it against the smaller lid; Thorn moved quickly beside him, getting his fingers beneath the lid as Jennings fiercely pried up. In a single movement it was off and Thorn's face contorted with grief. Within the small casket were the remains of a human child, its delicate skull smashed to pieces.

"Its head . . ." sobbed Thorn.

". . . God . . ."

"They killed it!"

"Let's get out of here."

"They murdered my son!" Thorn screamed, and the lid slammed shut, the two men's eyes locked in horror.

"They murdered him!" wailed Thorn. "They killed my son!"

Jennings pulled Thorn to his feet, physically dragging him away. But then he stopped; his body jarred with sudden terror.

"Thorn."

Thorn turned to follow his gaze and saw, dead ahead, the head of a black German shepherd. Its eyes were close-set and glinting; saliva dripped from its half-open mouth as a vicious growl arose from somewhere within. Thorn and Jennings stood motionless as the animal slowly inched forward from the foliage until its full body could be seen. It was thin and scarred, an open wound festering amid clotted patches of hair on its side. The bushes beside it began to rustle and another dog's head appeared; this one gray, its muzzle disfigured and dripping. Then another appeared, and another, the cemetery coming alive with motion as the darkened figures emerged from everywhere, a pack of at least ten, insane and ravenous, their mouths dripping in a continual drool.

Jennings and Thorn were frozen in place, fearing any movement, even that of looking at one another, as the growling pack held them at bay.

"They smell . . . the carcasses . . ." Jennings whispered. "Just . . . move . . . back."

Barely breathing, the two men began to back up; the dogs immediately moved forward, heads held low as though stalking prey. Thorn faltered and an involuntary sound rose abruptly from his gut; Jennings gripped him, trying to restore calm.

"Don't run . . . they just want . . . the corpses . . ."

But as they passed to two opened graves, the dogs kept coming; their advance unceasing, eyes rivited only on the men. They were closing the gap now, their fluid motion bringing them closer, while Jennings desperately

156

searched for the fence, seeing it was still a hundred yards away. Thorn stumbled again and clung tightly to Jennings, both men shaking as they struggled to back away. Then their backs hit something solid and Thorn shuddered. They were at the base of the great stone idol, trapped there as the dogs spread slowly around them, blocking any chance of escape. For an awful moment all remained frozen, predators and prey, the circle of dripping teeth holding them at bay. The sun was out now, casting a reddish glow upon the headstones; the dogs and men were held in place as though awaiting a signal to set them into motion. The seconds passed and they coiled tighter; the men rigid, the dogs crouched, ready to spring.

Emitting a shrill war cry, Jennings hurled his tire iron at the lead dog as the entire pack exploded into motion. The dogs sprang into the air, hurling themselves on the men as they turned to run; Jennings was brought down immediately as the animals lunged for his neck. He rolled as they attacked him, his camera straps wrapping tightly about his neck, tearing into it, as the animals danced around him, trying to reach the flesh below. Flailing helplessly against them, he felt his camera beneath his chin, its lens shattering as teeth viciously slashed at it, trying to rip it away.

They had let Thorn run farther, but as he neared the fence a large animal leapt upon him, its jaws connecting squarely with the flesh of his back. Thorn struggled to continue, but the animal hung on, its front legs dangling in the air. Thorn fell to his knees, straining to pull himself forward, while others descended upon him, blocking his view. Teeth flashed and saliva spewed into the air, Thorn crying out as he fought desperately against them, still trying to make it to the fence. But it was no use. He rolled into a ball; feeling hot, stinging pains as their teeth sank into his back. For a moment, he saw Jennings, spinning and rolling, the dogs repeatedly lunging for his neck. Thorn no longer felt pain, only the fierce need to escape. He raised himself on all fours again, the dogs hanging onto his back as he inched his way toward the fence. His hand came down on something cold. It was the tire iron that Jennings had thrown; he gripped it tightly, jamming it down behind him toward the animals tearing his back. From the wail of agony he knew he'd hit a mark, a gush of blood spurting over his head as a dog spun before him, its eyeball hanging by bloody threads from the socket. It gave Thorn courage; he jabbed hard again, then began swinging the tire iron with both hands as he struggled to regain his footing.

Jennings rolled over and over until he reached the base of a tree, fighting to pull himself upward as the dogs raged about him, still striking at the camera and straps wound about his neck. As he fought them, the flash attachment went off, and the animals cowered before the blinding spark of light.

Thorn was on his feet now, swinging wildly with the tire iron, connecting with heads and muzzles as he staggered backward toward the fence. Jennings had leapt from the tree, holding the flash attachment in front of him, triggering it each time the dogs advanced, driving them back until he too had made it to the fence.

He moved quickly to Thorn, keeping the dogs at bay while Thorn began to climb over. His clothes torn, his face bloodied, Thorn struggled upward on the fence, suddenly falling hard upon the top of it, and impaling himself through the armpit with one of the rusted spikes. Crying out in pain, he forced himself upward and fell hard to the earth on the other side. Jennings followed, triggering his flash as he went, then throwing it at the howling dogs as he jumped down on the other side. Thorn was staggering as Jennings grabbed him, half carrying him toward the cab, the cabdriver gazed groggily out at them, then gave of moan of horror. He reached for the ignition, but the keys were gone. He raced out, helping Jennings load Thorn into the back seat of the car. As Jennings ran to the trunk to retrieve the car keys, he glanced back at the dogs, which were now going wild. They were smashing themselves into the fence, howling with anger; one of them tried to leap over and almost made it, but was impaled by the neck, blood shooting out like a fountain. In their frenzy the other dogs leapt upon him, eating him alive as his legs kicked wildly and his voice wailed with rage.

The cab sped away with its back door flapping open, the driver shocked as he gazed into his mirror at the two men in the back. They no longer looked like men, but tangled masses of blood and clothing. And they clung to each other, weeping like children.

Chapter Eleven

The cabdriver had taken them to a hospital emergency room, removed their baggage from the car, and then sped away. Thorn was dazed so Jennings answered all questions, giving false identities and a story that seemingly satisfied the hospital authorities. They had been drunk, he said, and wandered onto private property marked with warning notices that the premises were patrolled by dogs. It was on the outskirts of Rome, but he could not remember where; just that there was a high fence with spikes that his friend had fallen upon. Both were treated for puncture wounds and given tetanus shots, then told to return in a week for blood tests to make sure the injections had done the job. They changed their clothing and left, finding their way to a small hotel and signing in under false names; the concierge insisted they pay in advance and gave them the key to a single room.

Thorn was on the phone now, desperately trying to reach Katherine, as Jennings paced the room.

"They could have killed you, and they didn't," Jennings said fearfully. "It was *me* they were after, they kept going for my *neck*."

Thorn lifted his arm to silence Jennings; a dark stain of blood showed through his shirt.

"Do you hear what I'm telling you, Thorn?! They were going for my *neck*!"

"Is this the hospital?" Thorn asked into the phone. "Yes, she's in room 4A."

"My God, if I hadn't had these cameras . . ." Jennings continued.

"Would you interrupt please? This is an emergency."

"We've got to *do* something, Thorn. Do you hear me?"

Thorn turned to Jennings, eyeing the strap marks on his neck.

"Find the town of Meggido," he said softly.

"How the hell am I going to find . . ."

"I don't know. Go to a library."

"A library! Jesus Christ!"

"Helló?" Thorn asked into the phone. "Katherine?"

In her hospital bed, Katherine moved to an upright position, concerned by the urgency in her husband's voice. She held the phone with her good hand, the other immobilized by the angular cast.

"Are you all right?" Thorn asked desperately.

"Yes. Are you?"

"Yes. I just wanted to make sure . . ."

"Where are you?"

"I'm in Rome. A hotel called the Imperatore."

"What's wrong?"

"Nothing."

"Are you ill?"

"No, I was worried . . ."

"Come back, Jerry."

"I can't come back right now."

"I'm frightened."

"There's nothing to be frightened of."

"I've been calling the house and there's no answer."

In his hotel room, Thorn looked at Jennings who was changing his shirt, preparing to go out.

"Jerry?" said Katherine. "I think I'd better go home."

"Stay where you are." Thorn warned.

"I'm worried about Damien."

"Don't go near the house, Katherine.

"I *have* to . . ."

"Listen to me, Katherine. Don't go near the house."

Katherine stopped, alarmed by his tone.

"If you're worried about my doing something," she

said, "you don't have to be. I've been talking to the psychiatrist, and I see things more clearly now. It isn't Damien that's causing any of this, it's me."

"Katherine . . ."

"Listen to me. I'm taking a drug called Lithium. It's a drug for depression. And it works. I want to go home. And I want you to come back." She paused, her voice thickening. "And I want everything to be all right."

"Who gave you the drug?" asked Thorn.

"Dr. Greer."

"Stay in that hospital, Katherine. Don't leave until I come for you."

"I want to go home, Jerry."

"For God's sake . . ."

"I'm all *right*!"

"You're not all right!"

"Don't worry."

"Katherine!"

"I'm going home, Jerry."

"Don't! I'll come back."

"When?"

"In the morning."

"But what if something's wrong at home? I've called there . . ."

"Something *is* wrong at home, Katherine."

She paused, chilled by his words.

"Jerry?" she asked quietly. "What's wrong?"

"Not over the phone," Thorn agonized.

"What's happening? What's wrong at home?"

"Just wait for me there. Just don't move from the hospital. I'll be home in the morning and explain it all."

"Please don't do this to me . . ."

"It's *not* you, Katherine. There's nothing wrong with you."

"What are you saying?"

162

In the hotel room, Jennings shot Thorn a look and gravely shook his head.

"Jerry?"

"He's not our child, Katherine. Damien belongs to someone else."

"What?"

"Don't go home," warned Thorn. "Just wait for me there."

He hung up and Katherine sat in stunned silence, unmoving until the receiver began to buzz in her ear. Slowly returning it to the cradle, she stared at the shadows playing on the walls, a tree outside her sixth-floor room swaying gently in the summer breeze. She was frightened but aware that the feeling of panic that always accompanied her fright was gone. The drug was doing its job, she was able to keep her head clear. Lifting the phone again, she dialed her home number. Again, no answer. She then turned to the intercom above her bed and struggled to push its button.

"Yes, ma'am?" replied a voice.

"I have to leave the hospital. Is there someone I should talk to?"

"You'll have to have your doctor's permission."

"Can you find him for me, please?"

"I'll try."

The voice clicked off and Katherine sat in silence. A nurse brought her lunch in but she had no appetite. There was a small plate of Jell-O on the tray. She found herself touching it; it felt cool and calming, and she kneaded it between her fingers.

Several hundred miles away, in the graveyard of Cerveteri, all was silent, the sky overcast, the stillness broken only by the barely audible sound of digging. At the two despoiled gravesites, two dogs pawed the dirt, their limbs moving mechanically as they refilled the opened crypts, dirt sprinkling gently down on the skeletal remains of the jackal and the child. Far behind them the disemboweled remains of a dog hung lifeless on an iron fence, while a lonely compatriot lifted its head and uttered a low and mournful sound. The cry rang throughout the cemetery, slowly rising in intensity; other animals joined in until the air was filled with the discordant chorus of doom.

In her hospital room, Katherine reached for the intercom, her voice edged with impatience.

"Is anyone there?" she asked.

"Yes?" a voice answered.

"I asked you to locate my doctor."

"I'm afraid I can't. He might be in surgery."

Katherine's face was taut with irritation.

"Could you come in here and help me, please?"

"I'll try to send somebody in."

"Please hurry."

"I'll do my best."

She struggled to get out of bed, moving to the wardrobe where she quickly found her clothes. The dress was like a smock and would be easy to get on, but the nightgown she was wearing buttoned high at the neck and she looked at herself in the mirror wondering how, with the cast, she could get it off. It was purple gossamer, a ridiculous sight on a woman with her arm in stiff plaster. Katherine pulled at the buttons, her frustration growing as they refused to come undone. In a sudden motion, the buttons popped and Katherine struggled to lift the gown over her head, but she became ensnared in a tangle of purple haze.

In the graveyard the air rang with growing rage; in her hospital room, Katherine fought against the net of gossamer, winding it tighter around her head and neck. She felt an instant of panic and began to breath heavily, but then a door opened and she relaxed, knowing that help had finally come.

The graveyard of Cimitèro di Sant'Angelo reverberated with sound, the wailing growing to even greater heights.

"Hello?" asked Katherine, trying to see who had come in.

But there was no answer and she spun around, searching the room through her gossamer veil.

"Is someone here?"

And then she stopped.

It was Mrs. Baylock; her face powered white, her mouth set in a lipstick-painted grin. Speechless, Katherine watched as the woman walked slowly past her and threw open the window, gazing down into the street below.

"Could you help me . . . ?" Katherine whispered. "I seem . . . to be stuck in here."

Mrs. Baylock merely grinned; Katherine weakened at the sight of her face.

"It's a beautiful day, Katherine," the woman said. "A beautiful day for flying."

And she moved forward, gripping the nightgown tightly in her fists.

"Please . . ." Katherine pleaded.

Their eyes held for one long, last moment.

"You look so beautiful," Mrs. Baylock said. "Give us a kiss."

She leaned forward and Katherine lurched back, the woman spinning her violently toward the window.

In the hospital emergency entrance, an ambulance screeched in, its siren screaming and red light twirling, as high above in a sixth-story window the figure of a woman with a purple nightgown wrapped about her face gracefully took flight. The figure revolved slowly in its long descent, the movement of its cast forming a design in the air. No one saw it until the body hit the roof of the ambulance, bouncing upward for a final flight before coming to rest, dead, in the emergency entrance driveway.

There was silence now at Cerveteri; the graves covered, the dogs vanished into the thicket.

165

Thorn, fallen into an exhausted sleep, was awakened by the phone. It was dark now, and Jennings was gone.

"Yes?" Thorn answered groggily.

It was Dr. Becker; the tone of his voice betrayed the news to come.

"I'm glad I found you," he said. "The name of the hotel was written on Katherine's night table, but I had trouble locating . . ."

"What's wrong?" asked Thorn.

"I'm sorry to have to tell you this over long distance."

"What happened?"

"Katherine jumped from her hospital window."

". . . What . . . ?" gasped Thorn.

"She's dead, Mr. Thorn. We did everything we could."

A knot formed in Thorn's throat; he was unable to speak.

"We don't know what happened exactly. She'd asked to leave the hospital and then we found her outside."

"She's dead . . . ?" whimpered Thorn.

"She died instantly. Her skull was crushed on impact."

Thorn began to moan and held the receiver against his chest.

"Mr. Thorn?" the doctor asked.

But he was answered with the sound of a disconnect. In the darkness of his room Thorn wept, his sobs echoing down the corridor outside. A night porter hurried to his room and knocked, but all went silent within and stayed that way for hours.

At midnight Jennings returned, his gangly form bent with exhaustion as he entered the room and looked at Thorn's figure lying on the bed.

"Thorn?"

"Yes," Thorn whispered.

"I went to the library, then the auto club, then called the Royal Geographic Society."

Thorn didn't answer and Jennings sat heavily on the opposite side of the bed. He could see that the bloodstain on Thorn's shirt had widened, the area beneath his armpit dark and wet.

"I found out about the town of Meggido. It's taken from the word 'Armageddon.' The end of the world."

"Where is it?" Thorn asked without expression.

"About fifty feet underground, I'm afraid. Outside the city of Jerusalem. There's an excavation going on there. Some American university."

There was no reply and Jennings moved to his own bed where he lay down, limp with exhaustion.

"I want to go there," whispered Thorn.

Jennings nodded, emitting a long sigh. "If you could only remember the name of the old man . . ."

"Bugenhagen."

Jennings glanced at him, still unable to see Thorn's eyes.

"Bugenhagen?"

"Yes. I've remembered the poem, too."

Jennings' face was filled with confusion.

"The name of the man you're supposed to see is *Bugenhagen?*"

"Yes."

"Bugenhagen was a seventeenth-century exorcist. He was mentioned in one of those books we've got."

"That was the name," replied Thorn without expression. "I've remembered it all. Everything he said."

"Hallelujah," Jennings muttered.

"When the Jews return to Zion . . ." Thorn recited in a near whisper, ". . . And a comet fills the sky . . . and the Holy Roman Empire rises . . . then all of us will die."

Jennings listened intently in the darkness; finally, alerted by the lifeless tone, he knew something in Thorn had changed.

"From the eternal sea he rises ..." Thorn continued, "... with armies on either shore ... turning man against his brother ... until man exists no more."

He fell silent; Jennings waited while the sound of a police car sped toward them, and passed on by the window.

"Has something happened?" he asked.

"Katherine's dead," replied Thorn without emotion. "I want the child to die, too."

They listened to the sounds of the streets outside and both were still awake at dawn when the sounds had fallen to silence. At eight o'clock Jennings dialed El-A1 and booked the noon flight to Israel.

In all of his travels, Thorn had never been to Israel; his knowledge of the land came from newspaper accounts of strife and his recent research into the Bible. He was struck by its modernity. A country that was conceived in the time of the Pharaohs but born in the age of asphalt and concrete, it was like a dollop of plaster dropped in the middle of an arid desert. The sky that had watched over exodus on camel back was punctured now with high-rise buildings and towering hotels, the sound of construction booming everywhere. Giant cranes lumbered like mechanical elephants, swinging their trunkloads of building materials ever upward, the city seemingly determined to spread in whatever direction it could. Jackhammers tore up sidewalks and streets already obsolete after so few years; signs hung everywhere offering excursions to the Holy Land. Police too were much in evidence, checking luggage and handbags, their eyes constantly on the watch for potential saboteurs.

Thorn and Jennings were stopped at the airport, their facial bruises arousing suspicion. Thorn used his civilian passport, passing unnoticed as an official of the American government. In their previous flight to Rome, with less rigorous security, the private jet had served their purpose. But here the key to anonymity was to travel and look like everyone else.

They went by cab to a Hilton hotel, then bought lighter clothing in the men's shop downstairs. It was hot in the city, the sun's rays amplified by the concrete, and Thorn's perspiration soaked into his bandage, bringing fresh pain to the wound under his arm. It was discolored and still draining; as Jennings saw him changing clothes, he suggested they see a doctor. Thorn refused. All he wanted was to find the man Bugenhagen.

It was dark by the hour they were ready. They walked the streets of the city, passing time until their search could begin. Thorn was weak and perspiring freely; they stopped at an outdoor café, ordering tea in the hope he would regain his strength. They had little to say to one another now; Jennings was restless, discomforted by the lifeless silence of his companion. As his eyes wandered idly over the activity of the streets, he caught sight of two women watching them nearby.

"You know what we need," he said to Thorn. "To get our minds off everything."

Thorn followed Jennings' gaze, spotting the women who were now heading for the table.

"I get the one with the moles," said Jennings.

Thorn eyed Jennings with revulsion; the photographer stood politely offering the women a seat at their table.

"Speak English?" Jennings asked, as they settled in.

They merely smiled, an indication that they didn't.

"It's nicer that way," said Jennings to Thorn. "All you have to do is point."

Thorn's face filled with disgust.

"I'll be at the hotel," he said.

"Why don't you wait and see what's on the menu?"

"I'm not hungry."

"Might be very tasty," smiled Jennings.

Thorn realized then what he meant, rose and walked away.

"Don't worry about him," Jennings said to the girls. "Anti-semitic."

On the street, Thorn looked back at Jennings. Seeing he already had his hands on them, he turned away, walking off into the night.

He wandered aimlessly, his grief washing over him like a wave. The pain throbbed beneath his arm and the night sounds were alien; he felt that if death were to suddenly take him, it would not be unwelcome. He passed a nightclub, and the doorman grabbed his arm, attempting to persuade him to come inside. But Thorn kept moving, unhearing, unfeeling, seeing the street-lights through blurred eyes. Far ahead people were filing out of a synagogue and as Thorn approached, he saw the doors were open, and he silently entered. The Star of David was illuminated on an altar, biblical scrolls beneath it encased in glass. Thorn approached until he stood before them, alone in the echoing silence.

"Can I help you?" asked a voice from the shadows, and Thorn turned to see an aged rabbi emerging.

He was dressed in black and walked in an arthritic crouch, his small, boxlike hat defying gravity as it stubbornly clung to his head.

"This is the oldest Torah in Israel," he said, indicating the scrolls. "It was unearthed from the shores of the Red Sea."

Thorn regarded the man; his aged eyes, clouded with cataracts, were filled with pride.

"The ground beneath Israel is filled with history," the old man whispered. "A pity we must walk on it."

He turned to Thorn now and smiled.

"Are you visiting?"

"Yes."

"What brings you here?"

"I'm looking for someone," replied Thorn.

"That is why I came here, too. I was looking for my sister. I didn't find her." The man smiled. "Perhaps we're walking upon her, too."

A silence passed and the man reached up, flicking out a light.

"Have you ever heard the name 'Bugenhagen'?" asked Thorn.

"Is it Polish?"

"I don't know."

"He lives in Israel?"

"I believe so."

"What does he do?"

Thorn felt foolish and shook his head.

"I don't know."

"It is a familiar name."

They stood for a time in the darkness, the rabbi pondering it, as if on the verge of recall.

"Do you know what an exorcist is?" asked Thorn.

"An exorcist?" smiled the old man. "You mean with the Devil?"

"Yes."

The rabbi laughed and waved his hand at Thorn.

"Why do you laugh?" asked Thorn.

"There is no such thing."

"No?"

"The Devil. There is no such thing."

He moved off into the darkness, chuckling as though he'd heard a joke. Thorn glanced again at the scriptures, then exited into the night.

Jennings returned early the following morning and spared Thorn any conversation about his exploits the night before. His only gesture of acknowledgment came as he urinated with the bathroom door open; he was urinating into his hands and washing his genitals with the urine. Catching Thorn's expression as he watched him perform this strange and repulsive ritual, he said,

"Taught me this in the RAF. It's as good as penicillin."

Thorn closed the door and waited impatiently for Jennings to dress. He was disgusted to be in the company of this man. But he feared being alone even more.

"Let's go," Jennings said, grabbing his camera bag. "I got us on a tour to the digs when I came in this morning."

They traveled on a mini-bus with ten others through the old city of Jerusalem. There they stopped at the Wailing Wall where the tourists disembarked and greedily took pictures. The commercialism even here was grotesque: vendors moving through the crowds of wailing Jews, shouting over them as they hawked everything from hot dogs to plastic replicas of Christ up on the cross. Jennings bought two such crucifixes, hanging one about his neck, giving the other one to Thorn.

"Put it on, old boy. Might need it."

But Thorn refused, irritated by Jennings behaving as though he were on a joyride.

The trip into the desert was less amusing. The tour guide recounted the recent history of warfare between the Arabs and Jews, pointing out the Golan Heights were most of the major battles had raged. They rumbled through the village of Daa-Lot where a group of Jewish schoolchildren had been massacred by Arab terrorists, and then the tour guide told how another group of terrorists had been captured and killed, their bodies trampled to pulp by schoolchildren in return.

"Now we know what all the wailing's about," muttered Jennings.

Thorn refused to respond and they rode the rest of the way in silence.

When they finally reached the archaeological digs, the tourists were hot and tired, complaining as the tour guide pointed into the roped-off area and explained the work being done. Beneath their feet were King Solomon's quarries, an intricate system of ditches and canals that possibly stretched to Jerusalem, some sixty miles away. Somewhere within the system were the ruins of an ancient city, believed by many to be the site where the Bible itself was created. Text had already been recovered, carefully preserved in pottery and cloth, that reflected stories closely following those in the Old Testament. The dig was an ambitious project, for no one knew exactly where the city lay; it was being uncovered, not with earthmovers but inch by inch, with pick and brush.

As the guide rambled on, Jennings and Thorn sought out some of the archaeological students, but gleaned little information. They were unfamiliar with the name "Bugenhagen," and all they knew about the city of Meggido was that many centuries ago a violent upheaval had caused it to sink into the earth. It was an earthquake, possibly a flood, for they had found snail shells here, far from any known body of water.

Thorn and Jennings returned to their hotel, then moved through the marketplaces, asking everyone and anyone if they had heard the name "Bugenhagen." The name drew a blank, but they pressed onward. Thorn was now desperate and his strength was ebbing; Jennings did most of the legwork inside shops and factories, checking out phone books, even visiting the police.

"Maybe he changed his name," Jennings sighed as they sat on a park bench, the morning of the second day. "Maybe it's George Bugen. Or Jim Hagen. Or Izzy Hagenberg."

The following day they moved to Jerusalem, taking a room in a small hotel there. Once again they moved through the populace, searching for someone who had heard the foreign-sounding name. But it was still no use. They could go on like this forever.

"I say we give it up," Jennings said as he gazed out across the city from the veranda of their room.

It was hot inside and Thorn lay on his bed, bathed in perspiration.

"If there's a Bugenhagen here we haven't a chance in hell of finding him. And for all we know, he doesn't even exist."

He moved inside, rummaging for a cigarette.

"Hell, that little priest was on morphine half the time, and here we are taking his word as _gospel_. Bloody good thing he didn't tell you to go to the moon or our asses would be _freezing_ right now."

He sat heavily on his bed, gazing across at Thorn.

"I don't know, Thorn. It all made sense before, but now it seems crazy."

Thorn nodded and moved painfully into a sitting position. His bandage was off and Jennings winced as he caught sight of the wound.

"That thing looks bad to me," he said.

"It's all right."

"It looks infected."

"It's all right," Thorn reiterated.

"Why don't I find us a doctor?"

"Just find that old man," Thorn snapped. "He's the only one I want to find."

Jennings was about to reply when he was interrupted by a soft knock at the door. He moved to it and flung it open, casting his eyes upon a beggar. He was a small man, an Arab, aged and naked from the waist up, his eager smile accentuated by a gold tooth as he nodded with exaggerated courtesy.

"What do you want?" asked Jennings.

"You look for the old man?"

Jennings and Thorn exchanged a quick glance.

"What old man?" asked Jennings cautiously.

"They tell me in the marketplace you look for the old man."

"We're looking for a man," Jennings allowed.

"I take you."

Thorn rose with effort, his eyes locking with Jennings.

"Hurry-hurry," urged the Arab. "He say you come right away."

They traveled on foot, moving through the backstreets of Jerusalem in hurried silence, the small Arab leading the way. He was surprisingly swift for a man of his apparent age; Thorn and Jennings struggled to keep up, almost losing sight of him as he plunged into the crowds of a marketplace, emerging at the top of a wall on the other side. He was amused by their fatigue, always keeping twenty yards ahead of them, winding fast through narrow alleys and archways, smiling like a Cheshire cat when they finally caught up with him, gasping for breath. They had apparently reached the end of their journey, but it was a brick wall; Jennings and Thorn were suddenly afraid that they had been tricked.

"Down," said the Arab, as he lifted a grating, gesturing for them to climb in.

"What the hell is this?" asked Jennings.

"Hurry-hurry," the Arab repeated through his grin.

Thorn and Jennings exchanged an apprehensive look, then followed directions; the Arab replaced the grating after entering behind them. It was dark within; the Arab lit a torch, moving quickly ahead of them. He descended downward and they could make out in the dim light a slippery staircase made of rough stone. The street drainage had created a thick coating of brown algae that stank and made movement hazardous. They stumbled as they moved downward, but once on solid ground, the Arab surprised them by taking off at a sprint. They tried to run but could not get traction on the slick stones beneath them. The small man sped away, his torch becoming a mere pinprick of light in the distance. They were in near darkness, the tunnel narrow and confining, the walls almost touching them

175

on either side. It was like a massive drainage canal, or irrigation ditch, and Jennings realized they could well be traveling the intricate system of ancient quarries described by the archaeologist at the digging site in the desert. Solid stone and darkness engulfed them as they moved blindly forward, their footsteps echoing throughout the tunnel ahead and behind. The torch-light had disappeared completely now, and they slowed, realizing they were alone. They could not see one another but felt each other's closeness by the sound of their labored breathing.

"Jennings . . ." Thorn panted.

"I'm here."

"I can't see . . ."

"That bastard . . ."

"Wait for me."

"No choice," replied Jennings. "We've hit a solid wall."

Thorn groped forward and touched Jennings, then felt the wall in front of them. It was a dead end. The Arab had disappeared.

"He didn't pass us going the other way," said Jennings, "I can tell you that."

He lit a match and it illuminated a small area around them. It was like a tomb; the rock ceiling seeming to press downward toward them, its crevasses wet and crawling with roaches.

"Is it a sewer?" said Thorn.

"It's wet," Jennings observed. "Why the hell is it wet?"

His match went out and they stood in darkness.

"This is arid desert. Where the hell's the water coming from?"

"There must be an underground source . . ." Thorn mused.

"Or holding tanks. I wouldn't be surprised if we're near the underground quarry. They found snail shells out there in the desert; it's possible there was a body of water that filled it up when the earth caved in."

Thorn was silent, his breath still labored.

"Let's go," he panted.

"Through the wall?"

"Back. Let's get out of here."

They began to feel their way back, their hands sliding along the moist rock wall. Their progress was slow, and without vision each inch seemed like a mile. Then Jennings' hand hit an open space.

"Thorn?"

He took Thorn's arm and pulled him up close behind him. Beside them was another corridor leading off at ninety degrees from the one they were on. They had apparently passed it before, unnoticing, in the dark.

"There's a light down there," whispered Thorn.

"Probably our little Gandhi."

They moved into it, groping slowly forward. It was not another avenue of the drainage canal, but a cavern; boulders were strewn in their way, the walls jagged and spearing outward at unexpected points from the side. Feeling their way carefully, they crept forward, beginning to make out the shape of what lay ahead. It was not a single torchlight but a fully illuminated chamber, its shadowy shape containing two men who watched and waited for them as they slowly moved forward. One was the Arab beggar, his extinguished torch held loosely at his side, the other was an elderly man garbed in khaki shorts and short-sleeved shirt, resembling the archaeologists they had seen at the digging site on the desert floor. His face was serious and drawn, his shirt plastered to his body with sweat. Behind him they could see a wooden table stacked with piles of papers and scrolls.

Jennings and Thorn climbed upward, across a threshold of jagged rocks to enter the cubicle and stood there, dumbfounded, squinting against the sudden onslaught of light. The chamber was lit with dozens of hanging laterns, the shadowed walls betraying the vague contours of buildings and stone stairwells molded directly into the rock. The ground beneath their feet was hardpacked mud, but in patches that had been worn down by dripping stalagtites, they could make out the shape of cobblestones that once lined an ancient street.

"Two hundred drachma," the Arab said with his hand outstretched.

"Can you pay him?" asked the man in khaki shorts.

Thorn and Jennings stared at him; the man in shorts shrugged as if in apology.

"Are you. . . ?" Jennings was interrupted by the man's abrupt nod. ". . . You're Bugenhagen?"

"Yes."

Jennings eyed him suspiciously.

"Bugenhagen was a seventeenth-century exorcist."

"That was nine generations ago."

"But you . . ."

"I'm the last," he replied abruptly. "And the least."

He moved behind his table and, with effort, sat down; the light from his table lamp revealed a complexion so pallid that it was almost transparent, the veins seen clearly beneath his temples and balding skull. His face was taut, and it was bitter, as though he had no taste for what had to be done.

"What is this place?" asked Thorn.

"City of Jezreel, town of Meggido," he replied without expression. "My fortress, my prison. The place where Christanity began."

"Your prison. . . ?" asked Thorn.

"Geographically, this is the heart of Christianity. So long as I remain within, nothing can harm me."

He paused, regarding their reaction. They were apprehensive, even dubious, and it showed on their faces.

"Can you pay my runner, please?" he asked.

Thorn dipped into his pocket and sorted out some bills; the Arab took them and immediately disappeared from where he came, leaving the three confronting each other in silence. The room was chilled and damp, Thorn and Jennings shivering as they gazed at their surroundings.

"In this village square," Bugenhagen said, "Roman armies once marched, and old men sat on stone benches whispering rumors of the birth of Christ. The stories they told were recorded here," he said, pointing, "in this building, painstakingly written down and compiled into books we know as the Bible."

Jennings' eyes settled upon a darkened cavern behind them, and Bugenhagen followed his gaze.

"The whole city's here," he said. "Thirty-five kilometers north to south. Most of it passable except for recent cave-ins. They keep digging up there, creating cave-ins down here. By the time they get here, it will all be rubble." He paused, pondering it sadly. "But that's the way of man, isn't it?" he asked. "Assume that everything to be seen is visible on top?"

Thorn and Jennings stood silent, attempting to digest all they were seeing and hearing.

"The little priest," said Bugenhagen. "Is he dead yet?"

Thorn turned to him, jarred by the memory of Tassone.

"Yes," he replied.

"Then sit down, Mr. Thorn. We'd better get to work."

Thorn was reluctant and held his place; the old man's eyes moved to Jennings.

"You'll excuse us. This is for Mr. Thorn alone."

"I'm in this *with* him," replied Jennings.

"I fear not."

"I brought him here."

"I'm sure he's grateful."

"Thorn . . . ?"

"Do as he says," replied Thorn.

Jennings stiffened with insult.

"Where the hell am I supposed to go?"

"Take one of the lamps," said Bugenhagen.

Jennings reluctantly did as told. Glancing angrily at Thorn, he lifted a lamp from its ledge on the wall and moved off into the darkness.

An uncomfortable silence passed, the old man rising from behind his desk and waiting until the shuffling sounds of Jennings' footsteps had faded.

"Do you trust him?" Bugenhagen asked.

"Yes."

"Trust no one."

He turned and rummaged through a cupboard cut into the rock, withdrawing a package wrapped in cloth.

"Should I trust you?" Thorn asked.

In answer the old man returned to the table and opened his package, revealing seven stilettos that glinted against the light. They were thin and ivory-handled; each handle was carved into the form of Christ on the cross.

"Trust these," he said. "These are all that can save you."

In the caverns behind them, the air was still; Jennings moved through in a half-crouch beneath the low and uneven rock ceiling, gazing with awe into the circle of light shed by the lantern he held in his hand. Within his view were artifacts embedded in the hard-packed walls, skeletons half buried in rock that seemed to reach out from the outlines of gutters and steps that once fronted the ancient street. He moved onward, drawn deeper into the gradually narrowing tunnel.

In the cubicle far behind him, the lights had dimmed; Thorn's eyes were filled with fear as he stared down at the table. Before him the seven stilettos were planted firmly upright, forming the sign of the cross.

"It must be done on hallowed ground," whispered the old man. "The grounds of a church. His blood must be spilled on the altar of God."

His words were punctuated with silence as he studied Thorn, making certain he understood.

"Each knife must be buried to the hilt. To the feet of the Christ figure on each handle . . . planted this way, to form the sign of the cross."

The old man's gnarled hand reached in and, with effort, unstuck the knife in the center.

"The first dagger is the most important. It extinguishes physical life and forms the center of the cross. The subsequent placements extinguish spiritual life, and should radiate outward, like this . . ."

He paused, assessing Thorn's expression.

"You must be devoid of sympathy," he instructed. "This is not a human child."

Thorn struggled to find his voice. When it came, it sounded alien, hoarse and uneven, reflecting his distress.

"What if you're wrong?" he asked. "What if he's not . . ."

"Make no mistake."

"There must be some proof . . ."

"He bears a birthmark. A sequence of sixes."

Thorn's breath quickened.

"No." he said.

"So says the Bible, do all the apostles of Satan."

"He doesn't have it."

"Psalm Twelve, Verse Six. 'Let him who hath understanding reckon the number of the Beast, for it is a human number, its number is six hundred sixty-six.' "

"He doesn't have it, I tell you."

"He *must* have it."

"I've *bathed* him. I've studied every *inch* of him."

"If it is not visible on the body, you'll find it beneath the hair. Was he not born with a great deal of hair?"

Thorn recalled the first time he ever saw the child. He remembered being struck with the sight of its thick, glorious hair.

"Remove it," instructed Bugenhagen. "You'll find the mark hidden beneath."

Thorn closed his eyes and lowered his head into his hands.

"Once you begin, do not hesitate."

Thorn shook his head, unable to accept it.

"Do you doubt me?" asked Bugenhagen.

"I don't know," Thorn sighed.

The old man sat back and studied him.

"Your unborn child was killed as predicted. Your wife is dead . . ."

"This is a *child*!"

"You need more evidence?"

"Yes."

"Then wait for it," said Bugenhagen. "Be satisfied that what you are doing must be done. Or else you will do it badly. If you are uncertain, they will defeat you."

"They. . . ?"

"You said there was a woman. A woman who cares for the child."

"Mrs. Baylock . . ."

The old man sat back, nodding with recognition.

"Her name is B'aalock. She is an apostate of the Devil and will die before permitting this."

They fell silent; footsteps were heard in the cavern behind them. Jennings gradually materialized from the darkness, his face filled with bewilderment.

". . . Thousands of skeletons . . ." he whispered.

"Seven thousand," Bugenhagen responded.

"What happened?"

"Meggido was Armageddon. The end of the world."

Jennings walked forward, shaken by what he had seen.

"You mean . . . 'Armageddon' has already been?"

"Oh, yes," replied Bugenhagen. "As it will be many times again."

He unstuck the knives and meticulously wrapped them, handing the package to Thorn. Thorn wanted to refuse, but Bugenhagen thrust them upon him, their eyes locking as Thorn rose.

"I have lived long," said Bugenhagen on a trembling voice. "I pray I will not have lived in vain."

Thorn turned away and followed Jennings into the darkness where they had entered. He moved forward in silence, turning back only once to see the distant chamber. It was gone. The lights had been extinguished and it had melted into darkness.

On the streets of Jerusalem, they moved in silence, Thorn gripping the cloth package tightly in his hand. His mood was dark and he walked like an automaton, oblivious to his surroundings, his eyes fixed rigidly ahead. Jennings had tried to question him, but Thorn refused to speak. Now, as they entered the narrowed sidewalk of a construction area, the photographer hurried to keep up behind him, having to shout over jackhammers as his frustration grew.

"Look! All I want to know is what he said! I've got a right to know, don't I?"

But Thorn continued doggedly forward, his pace quickening as though trying to outdistance him.

"Thorn! I want to know what he said!"

Jennings moved into the street, grabbing Thorn by the arm.

"Hey! I'm not just some bystander! I'm the one who *found* him."

Thorn stopped, glaring into Jennings' eyes.

"Yes. You are, aren't you? You're the one who's been finding *all* of this."

"What's that supposed to mean?"

"You're the one who's been insisting on *all* of this! You're the one who's been feeding this into my brain. . . !"

"Now wait a minute . . ."

"You're the one who took those photographs . . ."

"Hold on . . ."

"You're the one who brought me here . . ."

"What's going on."

"I don't even know who you *are*!"

He wrested his arm from Jennings' grip and turned; Jennings grabbed him again.

"You're going to wait a minute and listen to what I have to say."

"I've listened to enough."

"I'm trying to help you."

"No more!"

They glared into each other's eyes, Thorn shaking with rage.

"To think I've actually been *listening* to this! *Believing* this!"

"Thorn . . ."

"For all I know, that old man is just some *'fakir'* peddling his knives!"

"What are you talking about?!"

Thorn held up the package in his trembling hands.

"These are *knives! Weapons!* He wants me to stab him! He expects me to murder that child!"

"It's not a child!"

"It *is* a child!"

"For God's sake, what more proof . . ."

"What kind of a man do you think I am?!"

"Just cool off."

"No!" Thorn shouted. "I won't do it! I won't have any part of it! Murder a child? What kind of a man do you think I *am*?"

In an explosion of anger he whirled, hurling the package of knives far beyond him where it hit a wall and bounced into an alley. Jennings paused for an instant, looking hard into Thorn's raging eyes.

"Maybe you won't," he growled, "but I will."

He turned and Thorn stopped him.

"Jennings."

"Sir."

"I never want to see you again. I disassociate myself from all of it."

With his lip curled, Jennings moved quickly into the alley, searching for the package of knives. The ground was filled with litter, the air ringing with jackhammers and heavy machinery as he kicked rubble aside, spotting the small package at the base of a garbage pail ahead. Hurrying to it, he quickly bent over, failing to see the arm of a huge crane as it swung high overhead, pausing for just an instant before letting loose the huge pane of glass held tightly in its grip. It sliced downward with the finality of a guillotine, catching Jennings just above the collar, neatly severing his head from his body before exploding into a million flying pieces.

Thorn heard the impact, then the sounds of screaming, as pedestrians ran from all directions toward the alley where Jennings had disappeared. Following them, he pushed through the crowd to where the body lay. It was decapitated, blood pumping outward in a weak, pulsating movement as though the heart were beating still. A woman standing on a veranda overhead pointed downward and screamed. The head was in a garbage pail, staring upward to the sky.

Forcing himself to move, Thorn walked stiffly forward, picking up the package of knives that lay in the rubble just beyond Jennings' lifeless hand. With glazed eyes, he moved out of the alley, finding his way back to the hotel.

Chapter Twelve

The return flight to London had taken eight hours; Thorn sat in dazed silence, his mind refusing to function. The fires that had once sparked thought—speculation, imagination, doubt—had now been extinguished. There was no more fear, no more grief, no more confusion; only the mindless knowledge of what had to be done.

At the London airport his package of knives was returned by a stewardess who had, according to anti-hijack precautions, held them until the flight had terminated. She remarked on how beautiful they were and asked where Thorn had purchased them. He answered in monosyllables, stuffing the package inside his jacket, and entered the near-empty terminal. It was after midnight and the airport had closed down; his was the last flight allowed in due to substandard visibility on the runways. The city was buried in fog, even the cabdrivers balking at his request to take him all the way to Pereford. It was disorienting to return to London this way, with no one to meet him, no one to drive him, and he was stung by the recollection of how it used to be. There was always Horton waiting with news of the weather; Katherine at home, with a welcoming smile.

Now, as he stood in the cold night air waiting for a private limousine service to pick him up, loneliness swept over him and chilled him to the bone.

When the car finally came, they moved out at a snail's pace, the inability to see anything passing by creating the sensation that they were not moving at all. It was as though the car were merely hanging in space, and it helped Thorn to resist the temptation to think about anything that lay ahead. The past was gone, the future unforseeable. There was only this moment, lasting an eternity until Pereford finally came into view.

It too was smothered in haze; fog swirled about the car as it came to a stop, depositing Thorn and his luggage in the driveway in front of the house, which was quiet and dark. Thorn remained for a few minutes after the car had left, staring up in silence at the house that once contained the people he loved. There was not a single light within, not a sound, and Thorn's mind tortured him with fleeting images of the events that had once gone on here. He saw Katherine in the garden, playing with her child, Chessa laughing as she watched. He saw the veranda filled with people and the sound of laughter, the driveway packed with chauffeured limousines belonging to the most important people in the Commonwealth. Mercifully, the visions faded and he became aware only of his own heartbeat, the sensation of blood coursing through his veins.

Steeling his courage he moved to the front door and, with cold-stiffened hands, inserted the key. From behind him he heard a sound. It was a movement, as though something were running hard toward him through the Pereford forest, and Thorn's breath quickened as he opened the door and entered, closing it fast behind him. He had the sensation he was being pursued, but as he looked out through the leaded-glass window of the closed door, he saw nothing but fog. The momentary fright had been born of fantasy. He knew he must keep it from happening again.

Bolting the door behind him, he stood for a moment in the darkness, tuning his ears to the sounds of the house. The heating system was on, rattling the aluminum ducts, the grandfather clock was ticking, punctuating the seconds that passed. Thorn moved slowly through the living room into the kitchen, there opening the door to the garage. Their two cars were parked side by side, Katherine's station wagon and his Mercedes. He went to the Mercedes, opened the driver's door, and inserted his keys in the ignition. The gas tank was a quarter full; enough to get back to London. Leaving the driver's door open and his keys within, he walked back to the kitchen door, pausing to flick the switch that automatically raised the doors leading to the driveway. Fog swirled in and for a moment Thorn again thought he heard a sound. Stepping inside he closed the door and listened. There was nothing. His mind was playing tricks.

Switching on the light, he observed his surroundings. It was all as he left it, as though the housekeeper had retired for the night, and all was well. There was even a crock-pot of hot cereal incubating on the stove to be ready by morning. It shook Thorn. It was all so normal, so inconsistent with what he knew to be true.

Moving to the counter, he removed the cloth package from his coat, laying out the contents before him. All seven knives were there, looking freshly sharpened, the blades reflecting portions of his face as he examined them from above. He saw his eyes, deadened and resolute, but he was aware of a sudden perspiration that came on with the sight of the knives. A weakness began to sweep upward through his legs and he fought it off, rewrapping the knives with trembling hands, tucking the package back inside his coat.

He entered the pantry, moving up a narrow wooden stairwell, bending low to avoid hitting the bare bulb that illuminated it, suspended by a shredded wire from above. It was the servants' stairwell and he had used it only once before while playing a game of hide-and-seek with Damien. He remembered at the time making a mental note to do something about the shredded wire, fearing the child might one day reach up and touch it. It was just one of many hazards in the old obsolete house. There were windows on the upper floors that opened too easily, leading to sheer drop-offs and balconies that were unsteady, their railings in disrepair.

As Thorn trudged upward on the narrow backstairs, he had the sensation he was living a dream, that at any moment he would awaken beside Katherine and recount the terrible fantasy that had played in his mind. She would show concern and reassure him with her touch, and the child would toddle into their room, his face fresh and pink from slumber.

Thorn reached the first-floor landing and stepped out into the darkened hall, as the confusion that had torn into him before Jennings' death swept over him once again. He prayed he would go into the child's room and find it empty, that the house was silent and dark because the woman had taken him away. But he could hear the sounds of their breathing, and his heart throbbed with anguish and despair. They were there, both of them, asleep; the woman's snoring punctuated by the lighter intake of the child. Thorn had always felt that in this hall their lives somehow intermingled while they slept; their breath meeting and fusing in the darkness, creating a oneness they never know in their waking hours. He leaned against the wall, listening, then moved quietly into his own room and turned on the light.

His bed was turned down as though he were expected, and he went to it and sat heavily, his eyes falling on the framed photograph of himself and Katherine on the night table. How young they looked, how full of promise. Thorn lay back on the bed and felt tears tracing a path from the corners of his eyes. They had come without warning, and he gave in to them, allowing them to flow. Downstairs a clock chimed twice and he rose, moving to the bathroom where he turned on the light and recoiled in horror. Katherine's bathroom was in a state of total disarray, makeup broken and spilled everywhere as though some macabre celebration had taken place there. Jars of powder and face creams were smashed on the floor, lipstick smeared aimlessly across the tiles, the toilet stuffed with hairbrushes and curlers as though someone had tried to flush them down. The scene rang with vicious anger, and though Thorn could in no way comprehend it, he saw clearly that it was directed at Katherine. It was done by an adult; the jars smashed with decisive power, the smears bold and far-reaching. It was the work of a lunatic. A lunatic filled with hate. He was numbed by it and looked up to see his reflection in a broken mirror. He saw his face harden and then he reached down, opening a drawer. What he sought was not there, and he opened a cabinet, rummaging around until his hands came upon what they were searching for. It was an electric razor. Thorn flicked it to A.C., then snapped its switch, the small object humming in his hand. As he flicked it off, he thought he heard a sound. It was a creaking on the floorboards overhead. He stood in silence, barely breathing, until it stopped. It did not come again.

Perspiration had formed on Thorn's upper lip and he wiped it off with a shaking hand, then moved from the bathroom and stood in the darkened hall. As he walked forward, the floorboards groaned beneath his feet. The child's room was beyond Mrs. Baylock's, and as Thorn passed her door he stopped. It was slightly open and he could see her within. She lay on her back with one arm dangling downward, the fingernails painted a shade of bright red. Her face, too, was made up as he had seen it before; whorelike, with heavy lipstick and powder, and now she'd added eyeshadow and rouge as well. She lay still and snoring, her mountainous stomach rising and falling, casting a shadow across the floor.

With quivering fingers, Thorn closed the door, then forced himself to continue, moving quietly to the door at the end of the hall. It too was slightly ajar. Thorn pushed it open and stepped in, then closed it behind him and stood motionless against it, gazing across the room at his son. The child was asleep, his face peaceful and innocent, and Thorn averted his eyes, not daring to look at him again. He tightened his muscles and drew in his breath, then moved forward, the razor clutched tightly in his hand. Standing over the boy, he clicked on the razor. It hummed loudly, seeming to fill the room. The child slept, unnoticing, and Thorn bent over him, his arms quivering as he raised the humming razor, touching it light to the boy's skin. A patch of hair immediately fell away and Thorn gasped at the defacement; white scalp showing like an ugly scar amid the dark, luxurious hair. He pressed the razor down again and it cleared a path behind it, hair wafting gently to the pillow as the child uttered a moan and began to stir. Panting with desperation, Thorn moved faster, more hair falling away as the child's eyelids fluttered and his head began to move, attempting to turn away. He was awakening now, groggily trying to raise his head, and Thorn felt a surge of panic, pushing the child's head hard toward the pillow. The terrified child tried to fight him off, but Thorn pushed harder, moaning with strain and revulsion as he forced the razor onward, shearing off more and more hair. Damien was twisting and turning now, the razor connecting in random hits, the child's muffled cries of terror becoming more and more desperate as Thorn struggled to hold him down. The scalp was coming clean, and Thorn sobbed as he bore down; the boy's small body kicking and lurching as he struggled for air. Suddenly Thorn's eyes went wide, and he applied the razor firmly, pressing down at a point at the back of the child's skull. It was there. The birthmark. Its scablike texture torn into by the razor and bleeding now, but clearly imprinted against the white scalp at the base of his head. They were sixes. Three of them, in a cloverleaf pattern with their curved tails touching in the center. Thorn reared back and the child sprang upward, sobbing and gasping for breath as he gazed at his father in terror. His small hands felt his denuded head and came away with blood on them, and he stared down at them, screaming in fear. He reached for his father and cried; Thorn was paralyzed by the helpless fear in his eyes. But he was unable to comfort him, instead beginning to sob as the bloodied hands stretched outward toward him, the child pleading for help.

"Damien . . ." Thorn sobbed.

But at that moment the door behind him burst open and he turned to see the gargantuan form of Mrs. Baylock hurtling through the air, her reddened lips stretched wide in an unearthly cry of rage. Thorn grabbed for the child but the woman landed squarely upon him, knocking him to the floor. Damien screamed in terror and ran from the bed; Thorn rolled beneath the woman and grappled with her hands as they dug deep into his eyes and neck. He hit at her, but her weight was too much for him, her meaty hands finding his throat and pressing until his eyes began to bulge. Thorn desperately pushed at her face, her teeth sinking into his hand as a lamp tumbled from a table beside them; he reached for it, bringing it hard against her head. It shattered on contact and stunned her; the woman shuddered and reeled to one side. Thorn hit her again with the broken base, feeling her skull give way beneath it as blood streaked down through the white powder on her cheeks and chin. But still she clung to him; Thorn hit her a third time before she fell sideways and he struggled to his feet, staggering backward to the wall where the child stood, his eyes glazed with horror. Thorn grabbed him and lurched out the door, rebounding off the walls of the hallway as he made it to the back stairwell and slammed the door behind him. Damien clung to the doorknob, banging on the door, and Thorn wrenched him away; the child's hands clawed his face as they half-fell down the stairs together. In mid-stairwell the boy grabbed hold of the hanging lightbulb and Thorn strained to pull him free; both suddenly were jarred by a jolt of electricity that knocked them over, throwing them downward to the bottom of the stairs.

Landing on the pantry floor, Thorn crawled on all fours, dazed, trying to get his bearings. Finding the child unconscious beside him, he tried to lift him but was unable, falling backward as he heard the sound of the kitchen door opening and dizzily turned. It was Mrs. Baylock, staggering forward, her head a fountain of blood. He struggled to regain his footing, but she caught him by the coat, spinning him as he desperately pulled at drawers that flew out of his grip, their contents spilling upon the floor. He too came crashing down, the woman flinging herself upon him, her bloodied hands digging viciously into his throat. Her face was pink from the mixture of powder and blood, her teeth caked with it as she snarled, her mouth opening wide with the full force of exertion. Thorn was helpless, choking, as he stared into her maniacal eyes, her face coming closer until her lips pressed hard upon his. The floor around them was littered with utensils spilled from the drawers and Thorn's hands reaching desperately outward, found a pair of forks and gripped them tightly in each fist. In a single violent motion they streaked upward, smacking hard into her head, implanting deeply in the temples on either side. She shrieked and fell backward; Thorn stumbled to his feet as the woman rose beside him, staggering about the room, trying in vain to pull out the forks that protruded from her head.

Lurching into the pantry, Thorn grabbed the still-unconscious child and reeled toward the garage door, bursting through it and stumbling toward the opened door of the car. He was about to make it when a sudden snarl rose beside him, a blur of black fur flying through the air and connecting with his shoulder as he fell sideways into the car. It was the dog, ripping at his arm, straining to pull him back out. The child had landed in the seat beside him, and Thorn reached for the door with his good hand, banging it hard into the dog's muzzle until blood flowed and the animal, howling in pain, let go, the door slamming shut in front of him.

Inside the car Thorn fumbled for the keys, while outside the dog went wild, leaping upon the hood and flinging himself against the windshield with tremendous force; the glass shuddered with each impact. Thorn's trembling hands found the keys but they fell from his grip and he groped desperately to find them while beside him the child began to moan and the dog continued to hurl itself at the now-cracking windshield. Finding the keys, Thorn reinserted them, but as he glanced through the windshield he froze with horror at what he saw. It was the woman, still alive, lumbering forward from the kitchen with her last ounce of strength, painfully raising a sledgehammer as she neared the car. Thorn turned the ignition, but the moment the car started, the sledgehammer came down, breaking a large hole in the windshield; the dog's head immediately came forcing through. Its teeth snapped and saliva spewed; Thorn strained back as the animal's face pushed ever closer. He was pinned in his seat, the teeth snapping within inches as his hand edged inside his coat and seized one of the stilettos. Pulling it out, he raised it high overhead, smacking it down firmly and directly between the animal's close-set eyes. It went in to the hilt. The dog's mouth flew open, emitting a roar of pain more like a leopard's than a dog's, as it writhed backward and slid off the hood, dancing on two feet as it tried with its paws to pull at the knife in its forehead. Its scream of agony seemed to shake the garage, and Thorn hit the gearshift, gunning the car backward. Mrs. Baylock staggered alongside the window, banging on it and pleading, her face a mass of pink pulp.

"My baby . . ." she sobbed, "my baby . . ."

The car sped in reverse beyond her, and she ran into the driveway and held up her hands in a last attempt to block its escape. It halted, then lurched forward; throwing gravel as it bore directly down. Thorn could have swerved to avoid her, but he did not. Gritting his teeth, he floored the accelerator; her desperate face was caught in the glare of headlights as the car smashed into her, its front end crumpling as she flew high into the air. As he neared the end of the driveway, Thorn stopped, glancing just once into his rearview mirror. There he saw the woman's body, a lifeless mound of flesh grotesquely twisted in the driveway, and on the lawn the body of the dog, silently convulsing beneath the light of the moon.

He gunned the accelerator again and swerved onto the road, rebounding off a rock wall as he sped toward the highway. Beside him the boy was still unconscious. Thorn jammed the gas pedal to the floor as he found the highway and headed toward London. Dawn was coming, the fog was beginning to lift. Thorn's car took the empty road like a jet plane on a runway. It fairly flew; the dividing line blurred directly beneath it as it whined in ever-growing acceleration.

Beside Thorn, the boy was coming around, beginning to move now and whimper with pain. Thorn riveted his attention to the road, trying to shut out any awareness of his presence.

"He is not a human child!" shouted Thorn through clenched teeth. "He is not a human child!"

And he sped forward, the boy groaning beside him, but unable to regain his senses.

The turn-off at West-10 came too fast. Thorn skidded out of control, careening sideways onto the off-ramp, the movement throwing Damien to the floor.

They were heading toward All Saints Church. Thorn could make out its towering spires ahead, but the boy had been jostled into wakefulness and stared up at him with innocence in his eyes.

"Don't look at me . . ." groaned Thorn.

"I hurt . . ." the child whimpered.

"Don't look at me!"

And the child obeyed, casting his eyes to the floor. The car tires squealed as they rounded a corner heading fast toward the church, but as Thorn glanced up, he saw a sudden darkening in the sky above. It was as though it had turned night again, a canopy of darkness moving in with sudden force, sparked with lightning that began to strike viciously toward the ground.

"Daddy . . ." Damien whimpered.

"Don't!"

"I'm sick."

And he began to vomit. Thorn cried out to drown the sound of the boy's pain. Rain came in a violent downpour; wind whipped up and blew debris into the windshield as the car lurched to a stop in front of the church and Thorn threw open the door. Grabbing Damien by the collar of his pajamas, he pulled him across the seat, but the boy began to kick and scream, his legs making contact with Thorn's stomach, propelling him backward onto the street. Thorn lunged in, grabbing a foot, and dragged the child outward, but Damien slipped from his grip and began to run. Thorn raced after him, catching him by the pajama top and bringing him down hard to the pavement. Overhead, the sky exploded with thunder, a finger of lightning hitting close to the car, and Damien spun on the wet pavement, once again eluding Thorn's hands. He leapt upon the boy, trapping him beneath him, then grabbed him around the chest; the child kicked and screamed as they staggered toward the church.

Across the street a window opened and a man cried

out, but Thorn continued on through the driving rain, his face a mask of terror as he struggled to make it to the massive front steps of the church. A howling wind rose up around them, hitting Thorn square in the face, holding him in place as he leaned in, struggling inch by inch to move forward. The child spun in his arms and bit into his neck; Thorn screamed in pain as he fought to continue. Over the thunder came the sound of a police siren, and from the window across the street a man's voice shouted desperately for Thorn to let the child go. But he was unhearing, moving ever closer to the stairs as the wind howled around him and the boy tore at the flesh of his face. A finger plunged into his eye socket and Thorn fell to his knees, clinging hard as he dragged the struggling child to the threshold of the stairs. Lightning seared down, ripping a path of asphalt as it shot toward them, but it stopped. Thorn was on the stairs now, pulling with every ounce of strength to drag the screaming child upward. But he could not. His strength was ebbing and the child's was growing; fingernails raked across Thorn's eyes, knees pummeled into his stomach as he gasped and fought to hold on. With superhuman strength he forced the child to the ground and reached into his coat, fumbling with the package of knives. With a blood-curdling cry Damien kicked it from his hand and the stilettos scattered onto the stairs around them. Thorn grabbed one while trying to hold the child in place. The police siren reached its apex and stopped, the child screaming as Thorn raised the stiletto high above him.

"Stop!" shouted a voice from the street, and two policemen emerged from the rain, one drawing a revolver as they ran from their car. Thorn glanced up at them, then down at the child, and with a sudden cry of rage plunged the knife downward, the child's scream coming simultaneously with the sound of a gunshot.

For a moment, everything was frozen: the policemen immobile, Thorn sitting stiffly on the steps of the church with the body of the child stretched before him. Then the church doors swung open and a priest stared out at the scene: a tableau behind the veil of down-pouring rain.

Chapter Thirteen

The news of the tragedy spread quickly through London, then onto wire services across the world. The story was confused, the details conflicting, and for forty-eight hours reporters crowded the waiting room at City Hospital, questioning doctors in an attempt to find out what had happened, and how. On the morning of the second day a group of hospital spokesmen filed into the room, waiting for television cameras to start grinding before issuing their statement. It was a South African doctor who had been flown in for specialized surgery from Groote Schuur Hospital in Capetown who made the final announcement.

"I would like to announce ... that death came at eight-thirty A.M. this morning. Every effort was made to salvage life, but the wound was such that its damage was irreparable."

A moan of sorrow went up from the assembled reporters, and the doctor waited until all was quiet.

"There will be no futher announcements at this time. Memorial services will be conducted at All Saints Church where the tragic incident occurred ... the body will then be returned to the United States for interment."

In New York City the line of limousines was waiting at JFK, the two caskets lowered into a single hearse that bore them to the cemetery on a crowded highway; motorcycle policemen forged the way. The cemetery was mobbed by the time they arrived; the curious and the mournful were held back by security guards as the official burial party was led to the open graves. A priest in flowing white robes officiated beneath the stanchion of an American flag, and taps was played as the coffins were placed upon the straps, a maintenance man testing the machinery and lowering them slightly just before the eulogy began.

"We grieve together today," the priest intoned, "for the untimely deaths of our brethren, two among us, who take a part of us with them as they travel onward into eternity. Let us grieve not for them who now go to their rest, but for ourselves who will miss them. No matter how short a life, it is a life complete, and we must be grateful for the brief time they spent among us."

The crowd was silent, some of them weeping, others shading their eyes from the sun.

"We say good-bye to the son of a great man . . . born into wealth and security . . . into every earthly benefit a human being could possibly have. But in this example we see that earthly benefits are not enough."

Outside the cemetery gates, reporters watched and photographed through telephoto lenses. Among them, a small group stood apart, pondering the confusion of the reported events that had led them here.

"Weird one, huh?"

"What's so weird. Not the first time people were murdered in the streets."

"What about the guy who saw them fighting on the stairs? The guy who called the police?"

"He was a drunk. They tested him for blood alcohol and it was loaded."

"I don't know," said the third. "Sounds funny to me. What were they doing at the church at that hour?"

"His wife died, maybe they were going to pray."

"What kind of sickies would commit murder on the steps of a church?"

"The world's full of 'em. Believe me."

"I don't know," reiterated the first. "Sounds like something's been hushed up."

"Wouldn't be the first time."

"Or the last."

At the gravesite the two caskets were being slowly lowered, the priest raising his arms to the sky. Among the assembled mourners were the figures of a couple who stood apart from the rest, surrounded by men in plainclothes, whose eyes furtively roamed the crowd. It was a man, dignified and stately, a woman in a black veil at his side, holding the hand of a four-year-old boy whose arm was cradled in a sling.

"And as we commit Jeremy and Katherine Thorn to their eternal rest," intoned the priest, "we turn our eyes to their child Damien, the sole survivor of this once great family, now moving into the household of another. May he prosper in the love they have to give, may he assume the legacy of his father and become a leader of mankind."

From his position near the graves Damien watched the two caskets descend, holding tight to the hand of the woman at his side.

"And lastly, to you, Damien Thorn," spoke the priest with his arms raised skyward, "may God bestow his blessings and graces . . . may Christ bestow his eternal love."

From a cloudless sky came a distant rumble of thunder, and the crowd slowly began to disperse. The couple surrounded by plainclothesmen waited until everyone had left, then approached the graves, the child kneeling before them in prayer. The crowds turned and watched, many weeping openly; the child finally rose and, with his new parents, moved slowly away. The plainclothesmen formed a circle around them, escorting them from the gravesite into the Presidential limousine.

Four motorcycle policemen escorted the limousine out past the line of reporters and they snapped photographs of the child's face as it stared back at them through the rear window of the departing automobile. For all, the photographs would be marred by a blemish, a flaw in the film emulsion creating a haze that hung over the car.